MARRYING THE MOUNTAIN MAN'S BEST FRIEND

BROTHERS OF SAPPHIRE RANCH
BOOK TWO

MISTY M. BELLER

Misty M. Beller
BOOKS

As the rain and the snow
come down from heaven,
and do not return to it
without watering the earth
and making it bud and flourish,
so that it yields seed for the sower
and bread for the eater,

so is my word
that goes out from my mouth:
It will not return to me empty,
but will accomplish what I desire
and achieve the purpose for which I sent it.

Isaiah 55:10-11 (NIV)

CHAPTER 1

*a*n icy wind whipped against Two Stones's cheeks as he strode along the row of shanties, aiming toward the one second from the end. Callum Morgan lived there, and if the man's plans had played out the way he hoped, his daughter would have joined him here in Virginia City by now.

Two Stones gripped the leather pouch tighter. She must be a young woman, for Callum himself showed only a few gray hairs. Yet the man had said his daughter had suffered a loss, which was why she'd come to live with her father in this wild village of miners.

And also why he'd asked Two Stones to find such a delicate gift.

There weren't trading posts in these mountains that stocked blue sapphire pendants hanging on gold chains. He'd found the chain in Missoula Mills and a ruby brooch in Helena, so he'd had to go to the Coulter ranch for the right stone.

Sampson and Jude Coulter had worked together to cut and polish one of the sapphires from their mine, then fit it in the brooch in place of the ruby. Sampson had sawdered another gold loop on the brooch so it hung properly from the chain. The price wouldn't be cheap for Callum, but he'd said he would gladly pay anything Two Stones required.

This gift must be important to him.

He eyed the narrow shanty that was Callum's. One board had popped loose at the end, leaving a wide gap where heat must be pouring out and the winter wind blowing in. The plank must have just come loose, for Callum would not have left it undone for long. Especially if his daughter had come as expected.

Maybe Callum would finally take Two Stones up on his offer to help build a house outside the town, away from these rundown huts that stretched in a long mismatched row of loose boards. Each shanty shared walls with the structure on either side or behind, which allowed heat from their warming fires to spread through the cracks from one dwelling to the next.

The stench flowed freely between them too. And the noise.

Beyond the foul buildings in front of him rose the grandeur of the stony mountains that loomed in the distance, their snow-capped peaks reaching heavenward. This picture of two places so different felt like his own life—split between the serene village where his Salish family resided and the raucous, unpredictable world of the miners he traded for.

Neither was a home to him, never had been. The closest thing he had to a home was the trail between the worlds, and riding through these soaring mountains was where he spent most of his time.

He moved to the door and reached for the latch string, but then paused. Callum was one of the few white men he knew well enough that he could enter without knocking, as was normal among his people. But if the man's daughter had come, Two Stones should follow the white man's customs.

He lifted his hand and rapped on the wooden door. The flimsy barrier rattled. Perhaps he should have used a lighter touch.

A moment later, the latch shifted, then door pulled open to reveal the shadows inside. A woman stood there, her skin much lighter than Callum's. The shadows darkened her wide eyes as she stared at him.

She didn't scream, though, as some white women did when they first saw him. Maybe Callum had spoken of him, and she'd known he would be coming. Maybe she even knew about the gift in the pouch.

She didn't speak, not even a greeting. Just stared at him.

He dipped his chin. "You are Callum's daughter."

She blinked. Had he said something that should surprise her? Maybe Callum *hadn't* spoken of him.

Disappointment pinched.

At last, she spoke. "You know my father?"

The disappointment nudged harder, but Two Stones pushed it down. Callum must not have mentioned him, for surely she would know him if her father had described him even a little—a man of the People who dresses as a white man, traveling throughout the mountains, locating trade goods that were hard to find. He'd built a reputation for this skill. For his ability to seek out what others could not.

He nodded. "I am Two Stones. I bring what Callum asked me to trade for." He used his best English, clearing away as much of his accent as he could. Why he did so, he couldn't have said. He shouldn't want to prove anything to this woman. Especially if Callum—a man he considered one of his nearest friends—hadn't seen fit to mention him to his daughter.

"Come in." The woman murmured barely loud enough to hear as she stepped back, allowing him room to enter. "My father is hurt."

Two Stones stepped inside. Callum's injury must be what kept him from greeting Two Stones at the door. He would find something to help his friend recover before he left Virginia City.

The air inside pressed down on him—the scent of sickness. She'd said injury, though, hadn't she?

She led him toward the back room, where faint light barely filtered through the darkness.

"Two Stones." The voice rasped with weakness but held an unmistakable warmth. "Come closer, my friend."

Worry needled through his chest as he moved toward the corner where Callum lay on a cot, his face creased with pain. Two Stones knelt by his side. Only his face and one hand showed above the blankets. Were his injuries covered?

Two Stones met his eyes. "You are hurt?"

Callum glanced toward his right shoulder. "A small cave-in. Timbers hit my shoulder. Broke the bone, I think. Can't seem to get my energy back." His eyes held no strength. And the stench of sickness was much stronger here.

Two Stones frowned. "The bone is not mending. Will you let me see it?" He was no healer, but he needed to know how bad this was. He needed to know whether the man who called himself doctor in this town could help. It might take the touch of a wiser one.

Too bad this place was so far from the Coulter ranch. Jericho's new wife could help. God had given her the gift of healing in greater measure than any other Two Stones had met.

Callum's eyes drifted shut, as though he didn't have the strength to hold them open any longer. "Don't worry over me. But tell me, did you bring it?"

Two Stones swallowed down his worry. "I have it here." He held out the pouch, and Callum's eyelids parted.

He didn't lift a hand to take it though. Did he want Two Stones to open the pouch and hold up the necklace? Or maybe just press the gift into his hand. After all, the man's daughter was watching them from the doorway. Perhaps he wanted to surprise her with this token when they were alone.

Callum's voice finally sounded, more weak and rough than before. "Open it."

He pulled the string to loosen the tie, then lifted the leather flap and took out the chain and pendant. The gold setting gleamed in the dim light, and he lifted it up for Callum to see.

The man's eyes widened, and he let out a hoarse breath. "It's a beauty. Thank you." His voice had dropped nearly to a whisper but strengthened as he called to his daughter. "Heidi?"

The woman stepped forward, moving to stand by his feet. "What is it, Papa?"

"This...for you." His voice dipped again, losing strength.

Two Stones held the necklace and its leather holder out to her.

She studied the jewelry with wide eyes, but didn't reach for it.

"Your mother had one...like it." Callum's raspy whisper didn't tear his daughter's focus from the gift. "She wanted you...have it. But...lost in...the fire."

Callum had to pause for breath between words, and his daughter's gaze shifted back to his face, worry marking her pale brow.

"Take it. Please." Callum had closed his eyes again, but he was probably attuned to every sound that would signal whether his daughter accepted the token.

In the years they'd known each other, Callum had spoken a great deal about his life here in these mountains, traveling from one mining camp to another. He'd even spoken of the wife he'd had back east, how she'd died when their lodge burned in a fire. How much he missed her.

He'd spoken of a daughter who'd stayed behind, learning to be a woman from others. But he'd said no more than that. A pain had always settled in his eyes when their talk leaned close to her, so Two Stones hadn't pressed. Now, he had no knowledge of why she would refuse this gift.

Finally she stepped forward and took it from his hand. Her movement seemed awkward, as though trying not to touch Two Stones. Was she frightened of him? Or did he repulse her?

A shift from Callum drew Two Stones's focus back to his friend's face. The man was looking at him through barely opened eyes. "Wood. Will you...stock...?"

"I will." Two Stones always did work around the place when he was here. Restocking the pile of firewood outside the shanty. Refilling the water barrel from the creek. Picking up a load of supplies from the trading post. Whatever he could do to ensure Callum would have enough to manage for a while. Callum should know this without asking.

Two Stones hadn't planned to tackle such tasks until the morning, but perhaps Callum wanted time alone with his daughter now. Time to tell stories of her mother and the necklace that had once belonged to her.

"I will see to all you need, friend." Two Stones pushed to his feet. "Then I will return to sit with you." They'd developed a habit of sitting by the fire, Callum telling tales of his time in the mountains and the colorful men he'd met. Maybe Two Stones could offer stories this time. Something to bring a smile and strength to his friend. Warm food from one of the hotels would help too.

As he left Callum's side, he glanced at the daughter, who stood motionless by her father, the leather pouch and necklace still lifted in her hands. Her gaze was fixed on Callum, though, with an expression not easy to define. Worry, yes, but much more.

She was older than he'd expected. A woman grown, according to the look in her eyes, but the pallor of her skin and hair made her look younger than she likely was. No wrinkles anywhere.

He turned his focus toward the front door. He would make sure these two had warmth, water, and food, then he'd see to Callum's injury, whether the man wanted him to or not.

CHAPTER 2

"Sit."

Heidi's feet felt like blocks of iron as she stood near her father. He was so weak. How had he declined so quickly?

He'd already been injured when she reached him a week ago. He'd been favoring that right shoulder but said the bone just needed a little longer to heal. Over the next few days, it hadn't seemed to heal, and she couldn't tell how much pain he was covering. He clearly hadn't wanted to talk about it, and her time married to Winston had taught her not to press when given a command.

But yesterday her father hadn't risen from his pallet. He'd allowed her to send for the local doctor, but the man clearly knew little about actual doctoring. He'd left a bottle of medicine and taken some of Papa's gold dust in payment.

Today, her father hadn't even gotten up to relieve himself. And he wouldn't eat more than a few sips of broth. He wouldn't let her get the doctor again either, not that she could blame him there.

Something had to be done. What, though?

"Heidi. Sit...please."

His awful rasping whisper drew her from her spiraling worries, and she forced herself to obey. To sink to the ground beside his blankets. This hovel didn't even have a wood floor or proper beds. They slept on a stack of furs, using dingy wool blankets for cover. She'd been cleaning as much as she could since she arrived, but when she'd boiled her bedding with lye soap, the covers had shredded in several places. She'd not yet attempted to wash her father's. He needed new blankets, but the trading post had none left. Hopefully, next week's shipment would contain a few.

Her father's good hand fumbled over his chest, reaching toward her. Did he want to hold the necklace? It was such an extravagant gift—not something she needed at all.

Her independence was gift enough. And safety from Winston's family.

She held out the leather pouch and necklace, touching it against his fingers so he could take hold.

But he wrapped his hand around her palm instead. She moved the gift to her other hand so he could hold this one.

His grip was stronger than she would have expected. Coarser too, like rough-cut wood.

Still, she hadn't held her father's hand in so long. Not even at her wedding. He'd not been there to give her away, as he should have. No, he'd given her away from another land.

From *this* land. These mountains had stolen him long before that day when her name and her life had forever changed.

She pressed down the bile that tried to rise into her throat. Forced back the burn in her eyes.

Did her best just to enjoy this moment. Papa had apologized for leaving her when she was only a girl. For abandoning her to a boarding school when she needed him most. He'd moved thousands of miles away, stepping out of her life. At least, that was what it had felt like when she was only thirteen and heartbroken after her mother's death.

He'd said he thought he was doing the best for her, giving her the life he thought she needed. She'd not believed him back then, believing he only wanted to be rid of her. But when he sent her the letter inviting her to come to him in the Montana Territory after she wired about Winston's death, the chance to reconnect had brought a morsel of hope. And when, after she'd arrived, he apologized for abandoning her all those years ago, she could see he meant the words. He'd been heartbroken too, having just lost the woman he loved more than life itself. They'd both been hurting then, but now they had the chance to start over.

They had much time to make up for. Like this simple touch. The joining of hands.

His throat worked, eyes parting. His mouth opened, dry lips cracking with the movement. "Heidi...my girl." Even in that hoarse whisper, the words brought a new round of tears surging to her eyes. "I...am not long for...life."

She had to strain to understand him. Surely she'd not heard right. He thought he would die from a broken shoulder? The pain—and probably the effects of whatever had been in the bottle the doctor left—made him tired and weak.. But he wasn't dying, was he?

"I want you...to go...with Two Stones."

Her heart skipped a beat. Go with the Indian? To where? For supplies? It seemed unwise to leave her father here alone.

He kept talking though, and she leaned in closer. "When I...die..." He paused often to breathe, and rest. "Do as he...says. He's a...good...man. Trust him."

Dread twisted her middle. Papa really thought this was his end.

"You're not dying. And don't worry about me." She was finally getting the chance to build her own life. The way she wanted.

"You can't...stay...here." His chest barely rose and fell when he breathed. "Not...safe."

She kept her mouth pressed so she wouldn't argue with him. She could protect herself. And surely he wouldn't die. She needed to find a real doctor for him.

She gave his hand a gentle squeeze. "I'm going to inquire about a different physic. You'll recover. I'll make sure of it."

She tried to pull away, but his grip tightened. "No." He croaked the word, and it seemed to take everything in him.

She stilled. "Papa." What could she say to ease his fears?

"Promise me." He opened his eyes farther now, his grip on her hand still tight. "Promise me, Heidi. You'll go with him." His eyes were nearly wild, desperate for her answer. Despite his weakness, he'd infused his voice with strength she couldn't ignore.

She swallowed. She had to say yes, even if she didn't mean it. If she found a chance to build her new life in a nearby town, maybe she could pay Two Stones to accompany her.

So she nodded. "I will."

He held her focus another heartbeat, then eased out

a rasping breath. The air seemed to take away half of his substance too, leaving him only a shadow among his blankets.

"Bring...Two Stones...here. Please."

∼

*T*wo Stones dropped the armload of logs on the ground beside the stack, then reached down to organize them neatly on top of the others. Four more loads tonight at least. Then he could bring more in the morning before he left.

The door to the shanty opened, and he glanced up to see Callum's daughter standing in the opening, her expression tense. Had something more happened?

"He's asking for you." Her voice pinched as tight as the lines at her eyes.

Two Stones straightened. "Is he worse?"

She shook her head. "He thinks he's dying."

The knot in his chest twisted tighter, and he strode toward her. She stepped aside to allow him entry, and he maneuvered through the dark space into the back room.

Once more, the stench of sickness nearly smothered. Was it death he smelled too? *Lord, You can't take him. Not this good man. My friend.*

At least Callum knew Creator Father. He didn't

often speak of his faith, but his quiet convictions held strength. If this was his time, Callum would be taken to a far better place.

Yet what about his daughter?

He knelt by his friend's side. Callum looked like barely more than a corpse now. How had he dwindled this much in the time it took to bring three loads of firewood?

Callum's eyes cracked again, so Two Stones spoke. "I am here, my friend. What is it you need?"

The lines of his face shifted, like he was mustering the strength to speak. Callum's gaze flicked toward the doorway.

Two Stones looked back that way, but the man's daughter wasn't there. A wheeze brought his focus back to his friend.

"Heidi. Please...will you...marry...her?"

Two Stones frowned. He must not have heard right. "Speak the words again. I did not hear." He leaned closer, edging his head sideways so he could better hear and still study Callum's lips.

Callum blew out a hoarse breath with the first words, but they were louder than before. "Marry...my daughter...please. Make her...your wife. Take her...to live...in safety."

The air lodged in Two Stones's chest.

Marry Callum's daughter? Take her as his woman?

He'd hardly spoken to her. And he was an Indian, a Salish warrior. Though his own people rarely seemed to think of him so, since he spent so much time among the white men.

What kind of life could he offer a woman? And she'd just come into this land, and from a very different place. She wouldn't know his ways. Likely she wouldn't even want to enter his world.

But as he looked into Callum's eyes, the desperate fear gripped his throat. This was a dying man's last wish. Whether he wanted a wife or not, he could agree to take care of Callum's daughter. She wouldn't be safe in this den of rowdy miners. He could take her to his parents. She could live in the quiet village tucked in a peaceful valley.

White Bear and Running Woman would love to share their home. She could be the daughter they'd always wanted. A replacement for Two Stone's sister, who'd died when only a girl.

He wouldn't need to take her into his own lodge, not in the way of a man and woman. She would be safe with his family, and Two Stones could provide her with everything she wished for. A much better life than she'd have in this hovel, surrounded by men who wanted her for only one thing.

"Please." Callum rasped the word, his fingers grappling across the dirt floor toward Two Stones.

Two Stones gripped it in a solid clasp. "I will, my friend. I will take her to safety and give her a good life."

Callum clutched tighter, his bony fingers like a claw. "As your wife. You'll...marry her." He sounded like he could barely breathe, and he was expending the last of his energy with his desperation.

Two Stones dipped his chin and placed his other hand over their joined grip. "I will. As my wife."

Callum eased, but only a little. "Find Turner. He was...a preacher. Ask him...to speak...words over...you both. A real...ceremony."

Two Stones swallowed down the roiling in his belly. Callum was making too much of this. Two Stones would see his daughter to safety. See that she had a good life. Why did he wish the marriage ceremony to be such a significant part? "I will marry and give her a good life as my wife. Rest easy."

Callum's eyes opened a little wider, pinning Two Stones with their earnestness. "A real...ceremony?"

He had no choice except to dip his chin again. "I will find Turner and ask him to speak the words of promise. I will make sure your daughter is safe and happy."

Callum's eyes finally closed, the fire fading from his features along with the color. But he managed a few final words in that hoarse whisper. "I trust her to you."

CHAPTER 3

*H*eidi couldn't help the anger coursing through her from the request she'd just heard her father make of Two Stones, yet panic wove with the emotion, propelling her forward. He was lying so still. Almost...lifeless.

She dropped to her knees by her father's head. "Papa?"

He couldn't have died. Surely. Yet he was so pale. Unmoving.

She pressed her fingertips to his neck, the action bringing back a memory too fresh. She'd done the same thing to Winston. That time, part of her had wished for the worst to be true. She could be free from him.

And she *was* free now. Finally loosed to live the way she chose.

This wasn't the way it was supposed to happen. Father wasn't like Winston at all. She could be free *and* live here with him. She finally had a chance to start fresh with her father and she didn't want him to leave her. Again.

She forced herself to focus on the sensation under her fingers. Was there any movement? Anything at all?

Nothing. No thrum in his neck. No lift of his chest.

She gripped his uninjured shoulder and shook it. "Papa?" Her voice rose with the panic flaring inside her.

His head wobbled with the movement. Like he could no longer control his limbs.

She pulled her hand back and clapped it over her mouth to stifle a sob. This was happening too fast. She'd just found him. Just finally started to repair what had been broken eight years ago.

He couldn't be gone now. Not like this.

The next sob wouldn't be quelled, bursting from her like vomit. Her body wretched as tears flowed freely down her face.

She lowered her head to rest on her father's arm, covering her mouth to hold back her moans. The scent of sickness and death clung to everything. Too much like Winston. She couldn't bear it.

A presence approached behind her, and a hand landed on her shoulder. She ignored it, pinching her eyes shut. But when the grip continued, she looked up at Two Stones.

He knelt beside her, his expression grave. "I am sorry."

Her breath expelled in a sob, and she couldn't speak.

"I will prepare him for the burial."

She nodded, but only because she had to. In truth, she didn't want to prepare for anything. She wanted her father back.

$\sim$

*T*he weight of Callum's request pressed on Two Stones's chest, making every breath a challenge as he stood beside Callum's daughter at the graveside the next day. They'd prayed over the grave. Or rather, *he'd* prayed, at her request.

He'd like to use these final moments to remember the man, or maybe share his own pain with the Lord. But he couldn't wrench his thoughts from what lay ahead.

Callum's daughter turned from the mound of dirt and the cross marking one end.

Two Stones followed, moving beside her toward the shanty.

She walked slowly, as though she knew this was the time for words to be said. The cold wind whipped across the open land between this yard of graves and the shanties lining the edge of town.

He slid a look at her. She studied the ground, the skin around her eyes red. She wasn't crying now though. Some might honor her for holding back tears, but it did not feel right in his spirit.

Callum had loved his daughter. He'd been a good man. A good friend. He would be missed in this world, though he'd been welcomed into a much better land.

His daughter should mourn him now, as she had when he first passed. Perhaps she would let herself do so again in time.

The moment had come to tell of the promise he'd given her father. *Lord, give me strength.*

He swallowed to prepare himself. "Your father asked a promise of me."

Her head jerked toward him. Before he could check her expression, the intensity of her voice made her thoughts clear. "You are relieved of your promise. My father clearly didn't know me well." Her eyes flared, and her chin came up. "I don't need your name or your protection. I can care for myself. I came out here to forge my own path, not to subject myself to another man."

The weight pressed harder on Two Stone's chest, wrapping around his throat now too. She must have heard Callum's request. Or maybe she only assumed her father had asked Two Stones to watch over her. He should make his responsibility and his intentions clear.

He tried to meet her gaze, but she glared steadfastly toward the town ahead. He spoke anyway, keeping his voice kind and steady. "I do not wish to make your grieving harder. Your father asked me to take you as wife. This was his strongest wish, and he would not rest easy until I gave my promise."

She flinched, like she was gathering to fling angry words at him, so he pushed ahead quickly.

"I will take you to Turner, the man of God, as your father asked, but after that I will not act as a man with his wife. We will go to my people, a quiet village in a valley rich with game and all we want. You will be safe there. My parents, Running Woman and White Bear, will welcome you to their home. I will make sure you have all you wish. And you may live free of me. The only time you will see me is when I ride into the village to bring you supplies. We will be as friends only."

He paused, waiting for her to say something. But she only stared ahead, her eyes unfocused. Finally, the same words came out again, but in a much quieter tone. "You are relieved of your promise. My father didn't know me very well."

Even if she refused, that didn't mean his promise could be forgotten. Callum must have had a reason for pressing so hard for the ceremony.

He glanced toward the town. The shouts and music from the saloons had already started, though the sun had only just begun to slip behind the western mountains. A shot rang across the distance.

Two Stones's middle clenched. Gunshots sounded so often in this place that he'd learned not to flinch anymore. But tonight was different. Tonight, he was responsible for a woman's safety.

And this place would offer her nothing but danger.

Callum was right. Two Stones had to take her away from Virginia City. And marrying was the only way to do it correctly in the eyes of other white men. Even he knew this.

Maybe he could explain it better so she would understand too.

He took a deep breath, steeling himself to continue. "This town has men who will think you do not belong to anyone. That they can do as they wish with you. But if we are married, none will bother you. I will not force you to do this, but I made a promise to your father. And I give you another promise now—to keep you safe and to give you anything you wish. You want to live a life with no man speaking over you. Allow me to keep my word to your father, and I will give you this life in the village of my people. I will give to you and take nothing. Your life will be your own."

She studied him, her gaze cool yet piercing.

He met the look, doing his best to let her see she had nothing to fear in him.

At last, she said, "I think you are a good man. I see why my father trusted you." Her voice gentled a little yet kept it's determined tone. "Even so, I wish to stay here. My father is gone, but if I could speak with him, I would have him take back his request, to absolve you of the promise you made him. He's not here, so you'll have to accept it from my own mouth. You are free from your vow. You can go on your way. Thank you for being such a good friend to my father."

With a firm nod, she turned and strode toward the shanties. The ramshackle row seemed to sag deeper into the earth, as if sharing the weight of sorrow for Callum's loss.

Two Stones let her go, but he couldn't accept her words. Callum must have known his daughter would be contrary. That was why he'd been so insistent.

Two Stones would have to approach it a different way. Maybe with time spent in prayer, the Father would show him what was best.

~

As Heidi trekked along the main street of Virginia City the next morning, where most of the businesses resided, the air hung thick with the aftermath of a rowdy night in the saloons. She wrinkled her nose against the scent of stale whisky mixed with the sharp tang of sweat and cheap perfume that clung to the damp morning air. The distant sound of clinking glasses, punctuated by slurred curses, drifted through the streets, a reminder of the revelry that had ended a few hours before.

She'd blocked most of the noises out as she fought for sleep. It came in snatches, though waking and sleeping both held their own forms of misery.

She stepped off the boardwalk to maneuver around a man's body. He lay face down, but his slurred words showed he lived and likely had no worse injuries than a roaring headache.

A mangy dog limped down the road, pausing to sniff at a shattered whiskey bottle. When she reached out to call it toward her, the animal moved farther away, as if even it understood this was no place to linger.

Debris littered the dusty street ahead—broken glass, discarded playing cards, and even a lost boot. This place really was uncivilized. A far cry from the cobblestone streets and flower-lined residences in Savannah. Of course, behind many of those front doors lived men just as crude and vice-ridden. They only hid it better.

But surely good people lived here, too, decent souls who would help her find footing in this strange world.

She maneuvered around a rut filled with horse droppings and stepped onto the boardwalk..

This town certainly wasn't Savannah. But then...that was exactly what she wanted.

She eyed the businesses ahead for any sign of promising work. She'd planned to find employment soon after arriving in Virginia City, but then Papa had been injured and weak. She'd worried about leaving him home alone all day. Now...she had to secure something soon.

She would likely find an eager employer in one of the saloons, but she wouldn't stoop to that life. She already had to hide herself from the men when they began imbibing each day. Their calls and suggestive offers made her ears flame, but it was easy enough to tuck herself inside the shanty once the rowdies began filling the streets.

Now though, she had a clear path to search for gainful employment. Well...clear except for the trash littering the street.

As she turned her gaze from the mess, a figure stepped from the shadowed doorway in front of her.

She stumbled back before catching herself. The man stood tall and broad-shouldered, his leathered face bearing the marks of a life spent outdoors. He wore a buckskin vest over a white shirt, and his blue eyes glinted in the morning light.

"Good morning, miss." He tipped his hat. "You look like you could use a hand."

Why would he think that? "I'm fine, thank you."

"Are you new to town?" Though he didn't take a step, it seemed like he edged closer. "I don't recognize you."

"I am new." Should she mention her job search? He wasn't dirty enough to be a miner and didn't have the look of a saloon owner. Nor did he seem intoxicated. Maybe he owned one of the respectable businesses— the trading post or the dry goods store. Or maybe the exchange. This could be her chance to begin her search. "I'm looking for work." Should she qualify the comment by mentioning the types of jobs she would be willing to do? They could be summed up in a single word— respectable.

"Well, I might be able to help with that." The corners of his mouth tipped in a friendly expression. "I've been looking for a bright young woman. What experience do you have?"

She swallowed. "I'm quite capable of running a household with servants. But I'm also happy to do menial tasks, such as cooking or sewing or assisting customers." She managed a pleasant smile.

His lips pressed together and he tapped his chin, his brow gathering as he thought. "I do need someone who's good with customers. A woman willing to do whatever is necessary to ensure they're pleased with our service." He frowned as he studied her. The look was so severe, she almost couldn't bring herself to ask what kind of business he owned.

But that *was* an important detail. She squared her shoulders and lifted her chin.

Before she could open her mouth to speak, he straightened and snapped his fingers. "I think you'll do. Can you start right now?"

She blinked. "Now?" What kind of business would have her start immediately without even discussing wages or details of the job? But if she would be working in daylight hours, it wasn't likely to be anything untoward.

Still... She offered a pleasant expression. "What type of work will I be doing?"

The man's eyes creased in a friendly smile. "It's probably easier to show you." He gestured for her to follow him down the boardwalk.

Her middle twisted, but she stepped forward. It wouldn't hurt to at least know the location. She had to find work, and she shouldn't turn down this opportunity until she knew for certain what it was.

But then he motioned her down the alleyway between the building he'd stepped from and the next. It was a path barely wide enough for the man to walk down without turning sideways.

She halted, her heart pounding faster. "Where are we going?"

"Just a shortcut." He looked back at her over his shoulder, his expression still friendly. "It's one street over. This will be much quicker than going down to the corner. Don't worry." But something in his tone set off a clanging bell within her.

She took a step back.

He spun and grabbed her wrist. His teeth flashed in a skin-tingling grin. "Come, now. Don't be difficult."

Panic surged through her as she fought to pull from his grip.

He was too fast, flinging her around so he stood behind her, one hand clamping over her mouth and the other wrapping around her chest and arms.

CHAPTER 4

*H*eidi lifted a leg to slam her heel into the man's shin, or maybe even higher in his kneecap. Her skirts tangled around her boot though, muffling the force of her blow.

Before she could try again, a roar sounded behind her. Not from the man. From farther away.

Then he jerked her back...and released her?

She scrambled forward, spinning to see what had happened.

Her attacker was on the ground, a figure looming over him with hands wrapped around his throat.

Two Stones.

Heidi's heart hammered as she backed farther away, onto the edge of the main street.

Two Stones glanced at her. "Are you hurt?" He was breathing hard, and fire sounded in his voice.

She shook her head, her own breaths coming in short gasps. "I'm all right."

He turned back to the man and released one of his hands from the cad's neck. In a fluid movement, Two Stones pulled a pistol from his waistband and stood to his feet, towering over the scoundrel lying on his back. "If you come near her again, you will breathe your last breath."

He took a step back, his gaze locked with her attacker's, even while the fellow scrambled up and away from the fierce brave. Once he'd gained his feet and retreated from the alley onto the main boardwalk, his eyes darkened into a glare so full of hatred, she took another step back.

Thankfully, Two Stones stood between them, his back to her like a mountain no man could conquer.

Just before the scoundrel stepped into the same shadowed doorway he'd appeared from before, his gaze moved past the brave to focus on her. "I'll have you, girlie. Ain't no injun gonna stop me." Then he disappeared into the darkness.

She wrapped her arms around herself even as Two Stones backed toward her, his pistol still aimed at the place the villain had last stood.

When he reached her, still with his back to her like a

shield, he spoke just loudly enough for her to hear. "We should return to your father's house. I do not think he will give up so easily."

Heidi shivered, the memory of the man's leering gaze still fresh in her mind. Two Stones was right. Men like him didn't take rejection well.

She started forward, retracing the steps she'd taken such a short time before.

Two Stones stayed at her side as they passed the building her attacker had entered, then moved behind her as she lengthened her stride to the quickest walk she could manage without drawing too much notice.

Who was she fooling, though? Her very presence drew notice. There were so many men in this wilderness city, and her father had warned that the few women here all worked for the brothels and saloons.

How had she ever thought she would manage to keep herself safe and find respectable work? No other female had been able to. Surely not all of them had come west already entrenched in disreputable careers. How many had been innocent, accosted by the man who'd tried to drag her down the alleyway—or another just like him?

By the time they reached the shanties, she'd begun to tremble. The awful event had passed. Two Stones had saved her. Yet her body didn't seem to believe she was safe.

She slapped the door open and stumbled inside, then paused to take in the dim room.

Her father's tobacco pipe still sat on the rough-hewn table next to the leather-bound Bible he'd read aloud from every night since she arrived here. Those last few nights, she'd done the reading while he lay in his bed pallet. On the wall hung the frying pan he'd scorched their breakfast in just a few days ago.

Heidi blinked back the burn that rushed to her eyes. She couldn't cry. Not now.

Two Stones entered behind her, and the door thumped closed. Quiet descended over them as they stood, side by side.

She had to face him, this man who'd risked his own safety to help her. Who'd appeared when she needed him most.

She didn't look at him yet, but she ventured words into the quiet. "Thank you."

"I'm glad I was there."

The feel of that man's grip around her wrist flooded back, but she pressed it away, fisting her hands against the memory. It felt too much like the things Winston had done early in their marriage.

She was no longer that woman, though. No longer the weak wife controlled by the men around her. She made her own choices now.

Yet, did she really?

At the moment, she couldn't stomach the thought of stepping out of this shanty.

Two Stones turned to her, his tone gentle. "It is not safe for you to walk through town alone." Something flicked in his eyes. Like uncertainty, but it disappeared so quickly she couldn't be sure. "Come with me. My village is quiet and you will find peace. I will not bother you there. And this will keep my promise to your father."

Indecision gnawed at her.

The picture his words painted sounded wonderful. A quiet Indian village where she could live her own life. She could learn to hunt and cook the way his people did. It would likely be vastly different from what she was accustomed to, but if it allowed her a peaceful life where she was fully in control, it might be quite pleasant.

But... "Will your people accept me? A white woman? Or will they wish me to leave?" She wouldn't go where she wasn't wanted.

He nodded without hesitation. "They will see you mean no harm. My mother will embrace you as a daughter."

The longing his words released in her would make her too prone to emotion, so she pushed it away. His village did sound like a good place to start this new life.

But what if it didn't work out? What if she wanted

to move on? "Will you make me stay there if I'm not happy? You say we would be married, but once we reach your village you won't bother me. What if I don't like it there? Can I leave on my own?"

His brows gathered, and a line creased his forehead. Concern filled his eyes, but was that sadness too? She couldn't let his emotions manipulate her decision. Not like before. She had to know she would be free to make her own choices if she went with him.

At last, he nodded. "I think you will like the village of my people. But if you do not, you may leave. I only ask that you tell me if this is what you want. I will not stop you, but I will see you there safely and make sure you have all you need for your new life."

How could she say no to that? This man seemed noble, but Winston had spoken pretty words to convince her to wed him. They'd all been lies—some he'd likely believed himself. But every one of his promises had been trampled on, over and over, by his own polished boots.

This man would likely do the same. But if she agreed to marry him, that didn't mean she had to submit to abuse from him.

In Savannah, Winston'd had all of society and the police department to ensure she remained securely in his grip.

In this vast Montana Territory, she could leave Two

Stones in the night and disappear forever. She would still be married and certainly wouldn't seek out another man. But she wouldn't subject herself to constant demeaning and punishment for offenses she didn't commit.

On the other hand, if he turned out to be speaking the truth now, she might reach a place where she could truly find the peaceful life she craved, a life where she would be free to make her own decisions.

He stood quietly. Not pushing. His presence solid, but not intruding while she worked through her decision. Was it because he believed he'd already won?

Either way, her chances were better with this man than if she stayed in Virginia City alone.

So she nodded. "All right. I'll come."

She could only pray she wasn't making the second worst decision of her life.

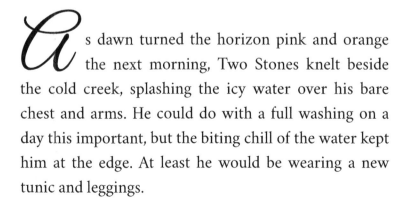

*A*s dawn turned the horizon pink and orange the next morning, Two Stones knelt beside the cold creek, splashing the icy water over his bare chest and arms. He could do with a full washing on a day this important, but the biting chill of the water kept him at the edge. At least he would be wearing a new tunic and leggings.

He'd sought out Turner yesterday after Heidi agreed to the marriage, and the three of them decided to hold the ceremony just after first light this morning. Turner could start his work at the mine straight after, and Two Stones and Heidi could head southwest toward the Mullan Road.

And home.

Home.

He always felt a little empty when he tried to use that word, even though his people had camped in that quiet valley for five winters now. It was the place he came back to when he had a lull between trips, though not as often of late. Still, was it home?

He pushed to his feet and slipped the tunic on, pulling it over his damp skin. Did Heidi regret her choice yet? If he gave her more than one day before the ceremony, she surely would, just like the others had.

This would be his third attempt at marriage. Neither of the first two betrothals had reached the day of the ceremony. He'd thought he loved Standing Kettle, but when her family chose another over him, she'd withdrawn her affections without a backward glance.

That had been a good lesson for him. He'd learned not to allow his heart to enter friendship with a woman. So when his parents tried to arrange a union between him and Yellow Mouse, he'd not been hurt when she refused to even look his way.

He'd made it clear to his father then that he would forge his own path, and that journey would *not* include a woman by his side. What would they say now when he brought Heidi to them?

And she was a white woman. Seeing that she was his choice for a wife would surely strengthen his family's belief that he was more white than Salish now. They'd not said such in several winters, but he could still see the truth in their eyes.

His chest tightened, but he scooped up his satchel and rifle and turned toward the shanties at the end of town. He'd given his word. He couldn't turn back now.

Of course, she would only be with him for this week they'd be traveling. After that, she wanted her freedom. And he'd allow her to keep it. In a way, this truly was the best situation for both of them.

God must surely have brought them together for this reason. *Thank You, Father.* Maybe if he offered thanks enough, this marriage living apart would feel more like a gift and not just one more rejection.

As he walked, he squared his shoulders. He had given his word to Callum. No matter his doubts, he would not break his promise. Heidi needed him, and he would be there for her.

Turner strode toward him from another row of shanties. As he neared, he lifted a hand. "Morning. Are you ready?"

Two Stones nodded as they fell into step together. "I am."

Neither of them spoke again until they reached Heidi's door. He paused to knock. Would he ever reach a friendship with this woman where he could be himself and simply walk in?

A longing slipped in his chest as he waited for Heidi to open the door. He *wanted* a friendship between them, like what he'd had with her father. Or maybe more like what was between him and Jericho Coulter. Both as equals, knowing each other well and accepting all parts.

As the door opened and Heidi stood in the frame, any thought of Jericho pushed to the back of his mind. How could he have ever compared her to that over-grown bear of a man?

He'd rarely been drawn to white women, probably because most of the ones he'd met were loud and coarse, working in saloons and saying whatever necessary to lure the men into handing over their gold.

He preferred a quiet woman, and he usually found them only among his own people. *The unfading beauty of a gentle and quiet spirit,* the Bible called it. A woman didn't even need to possess much beauty if her manner was kind and her spirit joyful.

Heidi Morgan had far more outer beauty than most. She was quiet too. But not, he believed, in a peaceful, contented way. It felt like more like intentionally holding back, afraid to be who God made her to be.

He offered a smile. Or what he hoped she would see as a smile. Many years had passed since he last tried to win over a female. "Are you ready?"

She nodded, any hint of joy leaching out of her expression, leaving her features pinched. Shadows under her eyes showed she hadn't slept well. Which weighed heavier on her—grief for her father's passing or being forced to marry him?

That thought would do him no favors, so he pushed it aside and followed Heidi into the shack to see what he should carry.

"We'll come back here to load the horses after...?" She didn't seem to want to speak the name of the ceremony.

His middle clenched tighter as he nodded. "After we are married, I will bring the horses here to load our supplies." He wouldn't allow their union to grow into a silent mountain between them. He would pledge himself to her before God. Whether she wanted him or not, he would do everything he could to gain her friendship.

They walked with Turner past the edge of town and stopped at a grassy area. The mountains in the distance rose up to the clouds, easing his spirit even as he filled his chest with a strengthening breath.

He glanced at Heidi to see if the view did the same for her. She was paler than usual, her eyes downcast and her posture rigid. Though she held her chin high in a show of courage, her fingers twisted the fabric of her dress.

When she saw him watching her, her features smoothed into a stoic mask. He could do nothing to ease her worries other than offering an encouraging smile as they faced Turner.

The preacher cleared his throat. "Shall we begin?"

Two Stones nodded, and Heidi must have too, for Turner opened his Bible and began reading the marriage liturgy in a steady voice that carried in the still morning air. Two Stones had heard this service twice before, and the meaning of the words swelled through him.

When it came time to exchange vows, Heidi's voice barely rose above a whisper. But she spoke the words clearly. "I, Heidi Morgan, take thee, Two Stones, to be my wedded husband, to have and to hold from this day forward, for better or for worse, for richer or poorer, in sickness and in health, to love and to cherish, as long as we both shall live."

To love and to cherish. Was she still completely set against those? If that was what she wanted, he wouldn't press her for anything at all.

But when he repeated the vows in turn, he spoke

them as a silent prayer to the Father. *Show me how to love and cherish this woman in a way that makes her feel safe and treasured. Without going back on our agreement.*

When Turner grinned and said, "It's customary for the bride and groom to kiss now," Two Stones wanted to glare at him.

The memory of that at the end of the other ceremonies slipped in, though. He couldn't shame Heidi by refusing, yet by the wariness in her gaze, he feared she'd bolt faster than a frightened fox.

He took one of Heidi's hands instead and lifted it to press a kiss to the backs of her fingers. It seemed the only way to keep his distance and still honor her.

The relief easing her face showed he'd chosen right, and the corners of her mouth even curved in the slightest of smiles.

Maybe this wouldn't be as hard as he'd imagined. The two of them might be walking into an unknown future, but if they worked at it together, they could make a good life.

He would do all in his power to make sure she never regretted choosing him.

CHAPTER 5

*F*inally. They'd put Virginia City behind
them.

Heidi couldn't even see the town now that she and
Two Stones had crested a slope and were descending
the far side. Clusters of lodgepole pines dotted this side
of the mountain, but she could see through gaps to the
long valley below.

Other than the clop of the horse's hooves and the
squeak of the saddles, the only sounds of life were the
occasional cries of a hawk circling overhead. Probably
searching for rodents among the trees.

Two Stones hadn't spoken since they rode past the
last mine outside of Virginia City. Was he lost in his
thoughts, or did he always ride in complete silence? She

didn't like much talking either, but she couldn't stand days of this.

Also, she needed to know more about what lay ahead in their journey. She could no longer follow a man blindly. That had become the only way to survive life with Winston, but she had control of her path now. If she chose to set out on her own, she needed to know more details.

When the trail leveled off a little, she ventured a question. "How far until we reach your village?" It was several days at least, but she didn't know exactly.

He eyed the skyline ahead. "A week." Then he slid a look at her. "My people measure time in sleeps. We should reach my parents in six sleeps." He turned forward again. "If the weather doesn't slow us. The sky speaks of snow. I do not know how much."

She jerked her gaze upward, pulling her coat flaps closer together. Already, the thick wool wasn't keeping out the cold as well as she'd hoped. She and Papa had planned to get her a fur coat from the trading post in Virginia City. She should have thought to do that yesterday. In truth, she'd not been able to think of much, not with her father's burial and then her impending marriage to a Salish brave. Even now, thinking those words made her situation—and her decisions—seem too ridiculous to even contemplate.

But as she glanced over at the strong, steady profile of the man riding beside her, a peace eased her spirit. She'd taken a step of trust with him. Of every man she'd ever met, he was one of the few who just might not fail her.

His voice interrupted her thoughts. "Before we reach the village, we'll stop at the ranch of my friends. The Coulters are brothers to me. Jericho has married a doctor, and she asked me to bring medicine from Virginia City."

She studied Two Stones as a flurry of questions whipped through her. The names sounded like they belonged to white people. A bond as close as brothers... how had he come to know them? And a woman doctor? That was even more unusual. Had she set up practice in the wilds of the Montana Territory? Apparently so, if she had sent for medicine.

Two Stones looked her way, drawing her from her thoughts once again. "We'll reach them just before Christmas. We can stay a few days if you wish. Dinah and her sister will be happy to meet you."

Christmas. How could it only be a week away? She'd been relieved to reach her father in time to celebrate with him. She'd planned to cook his favorite foods.

Two Stones still watched her, his expression a little hopeful as he waited for an answer.

She nodded. "Christmas with your friends will be

nice, if that's what you want. Will your parents want you home? Or...do they celebrate Christmas?" Two Stones had made it clear in various comments that he shared her father's faith, so that was likely why he observed the holiday.

But if his parents weren't Christians, they might want nothing to do with it.

He shrugged. "They do, but it is not the feast the white men have on that day. They are used to me sharing the meal with my brothers."

"That's good." She wasn't sure what else to say. Clearly, his faith meant a great deal to him, and familiar Christmas traditions would be nice.

The terrain steepened again, and she had to rein her mount behind his to maneuver the slope. Two Stones continued talking, though, speaking of the Coulter family. Six brothers, he said. Jericho was the oldest, the one who'd recently married the doctor. The doctor's sister and her young babe also lived with them, as well as the Coulter brothers' niece and nephew, who sounded like they must be school-aged. She did her best to memorize all the names, but Two Stones said little about what each was like.

Would the two of them be expected to share a room in that house? She could perhaps manage that, but what about the same bed?

The numbing thought stopped her breath. He would

introduce her as his wife, no doubt. Would he also explain they slept separately?

Her heart hammered, but she breathed a slow breath in. As long as Two Stones honored his promise and didn't try to touch her, she could manage. And if he did cross the line, she would have her father's pistol ready. She tapped her coat pocket, where she'd tucked it so she could reach it easily.

If he indulged in strong drink or some other vile thing that made him less trustworthy, she would be ready to defend herself.

$\sim$

*T*he first flakes drifted down an hour after they left camp the following morning. Heidi scrunched her nose as another crystal pricked her skin with an icy poke.

Two Stones had said he expected snow this day before the sun reached its zenith. Those were some of the only words he'd said during their quick meal before they'd packed their bedding that morning.

He'd been a gentleman through the entire experience of camping with him. He managed the animals and bore the brunt of the work to unload their supplies. She'd cooked a simple meal over the fire he made, but he'd carried the water for her, along with load after load of firewood.

Bedding down had been awkward, at least for her. He'd not shown signs of feeling the same. Because of the lay of the land, their blankets couldn't be on opposite sides of the fire as she'd hoped. But they'd been positioned end to end with enough space between them that she couldn't have touched him if she'd tried.

Once he lay down in his furs, he never rose again until the first gray of dawn lightened the eastern sky. She'd lain awake several hours, listening for any rustle that might signal he was coming to her. But that sound never came, and at last, her weary body succumbed to the call of sleep.

She kept her gaze on him now, riding ahead and a little downhill. Already, the flakes were thickening to a curtain, though each was still small. He'd not said anything about stopping when the snow came, so he must intend to continue despite the weather.

As they left the shelter of the mountain they'd descended to ride through a pass between two peaks, the wind picked up, swirling the ice pellets and sliding them into all the openings of her coat. She shivered as another gust crept down her neck, seeping into her bones.

Ahead of her, Two Stones raised his hand for a halt.

He reached around to the bundle of bedding he'd fastened behind his saddle. He must need to retrieve something.

Her horse shifted beneath her, stomping a hoof as they waited. She patted the gelding's neck. He must be one of Two Stones's animals, for he had similar markings as his mount and pack horse—dark coat with flecks or small spots of white across its rump. She'd not seen markings like these back east.

Two Stones pulled out one of the fur coverings he used for sleeping and held it out to her. "Wrap around you for warmth."

She hesitated. Use his bedding? The fur looked soft from many nights tucked around him. It likely carried his scent too.

But she'd begun to shiver more than she could control, and she would only grow more miserable as the snow dampened her wool coat. So she accepted the offering. "Thank you."

The pelt was even softer than she'd expected. She pulled it tight at her neck, snuggling into the comfortable warmth. It did smell of him, a familiar musky scent that made her feel safe and relaxed. Or maybe the warmth did that, but she was grateful as they continued their trek.

The snow began to thicken on the ground. By the time they stopped for a midday rest, at least a foot of thick crystals covered the trail, and the sky showed no sign of easing.

They'd dismounted to let the horses rest and now sat on a boulder Two Stones had wiped clean of snow. She handed him a biscuit and a chunk of sliced meat from their food stores, then bit into her own hard bread. It was almost too stale to eat, but she hated to waste food. Out here, there was no bakery on the street corner to purchase fresh goods.

She slid a glance at Two Stones beside her. Did he approve of using every last bit of food? Or would he rather have the best she could offer in this frozen mountain wilderness? As he bit into his second stale bite, and he didn't look angry or frustrated.

In truth, he didn't seem to be thinking about the food at all. His brow furrowed, his eyes staring through the snowflakes, his mind seeming far away.

"Are you worried about something?" The question slipped out before her mind had decided to voice it.

He slid a sideways look at her, a warm glimmer in his gaze. Not angry about the stale food at least. "I am thinking where to camp. We will not make the cave where I usually sleep." He turned forward again, his focus shifting back to that distant place. "I think better to stop at a cliff that hangs over." He bent his fingers at a right angle like a lean-to.

Heidi studied his hand motions. "An overhang?"

He nodded. "The snow will not cover us." Once more he tipped his face to look at her, but this time his forehead creased with concern. "It is not the place I wish to bring you. Not the way I wish to care for my wife."

A rush of something that felt far too much like emotion surged to her eyes. Such a tiny comment shouldn't turn her head. Especially when he'd only said he *wished* to care for her. He wasn't actually accomplishing that service. She would be sleeping in a snowstorm with only a rock overhang to protect her from the weather. Probably open on both sides for the icy night wind to gust through their camp.

Yet the concern in his dark eyes held her. Even when Winston had tried to play the part of the conscientious husband, his eyes had always given him away. That diabolical glint that lay just under the surface. But Two Stones...could that earnest regard be genuine?

She turned away, facing forward as she struggled for another topic, something to distract them both. "How much farther will we ride today then?"

"A few more hours. We will make camp before dark."

She nodded. "That sounds like a good plan." Dark fell early in mid-December, so they would only have four more hours in the saddle at most. Every part of her ached, though she couldn't tell how much came from the discomfort of so many hours on horseback, and what part stemmed from the aching cold.

They finished their meager lunch, and she was more than grateful for the warmth of Two Stones's fur around her. But the snow had begun to seep through her boots, chilling her feet. She breathed out her relief when he moved to her horse and led the animal toward her so she could mount.

Once they set out, Two Stones guided them through the drifts. She could see no sign of a trail, but he seemed to know exactly where he was going. How many times had he traveled this path?

After a few hours, they rounded a bend in the mountain, and the overhang he had spoken of jutted out from the cliff on their right. The snow still fell—faster now, the wind driving it into their faces in stinging pellets. Her breath clouded in front of her, and she could no longer feel her feet, though they'd been burning an hour ago.

Two Stones dismounted first and helped her down. The snow crunched underfoot, and she had to lift her boots high to push through the thick crust.

Two Stones kept his hand at her elbow as though she needed help to maneuver final steps. Perhaps she did.

His voice rumbled low beside her. "It is not what I would wish, but it will provide some shelter."

She nodded. "It's good." She would be grateful for any protection from this biting wind and snow.

Beneath the overhang, only a thin layer of ice crystals covered the ground. He halted her in the protected area. "I will make fire, then settle horses."

He moved back out into the snow to get the tinderbox and wood he'd said he carried for occasions like this, when the firewood around them was too wet to start a fire. She could make the fire when he returned. Perhaps she was being lazy, allowing him to do all the work out in the thick snow. But he was far more accustomed to this weather than she.

When he approached with the armload of wood and the metal box that held the flint and steel, he also had the other fur he used for sleeping. After dropping the logs to the ground, he handed her the pelt. "Sit and get warm."

She took the covering with as much of a thankful smile as her frozen mouth could manage. It was strange being cared for like this, as though he truly was her husband and not just a man hired to escort her. "Thank you."

She reached for the tinderbox. "I can start the fire while you care for the horses."

He handed over the container, his gaze holding hers for a moment, concern marking his eyes. There was something else, too, but she didn't look deep enough to identify it. The fact that he would put himself out for her well-being was unusual enough in her experience. She still couldn't quite trust it.

As he turned away and strode toward the horses, she remembered what she'd meant to ask. "Could you bring my satchel, the one with the gold clasp?" It held her two extra skirts and some hairpins, along with the gift she still couldn't bring herself to wear.

The sapphire necklace.

It had seemed so important to her father. Probably because it reminded him of her mother and that former life before their family was torn apart.

She'd done her best to forget that time completely though. To focus on the present and the life she wanted to build.

Maybe she would wear the necklace in time, but for now, it stayed safely tucked in the satchel.

As Two Stones nodded, then continued through the falling snow, she allowed herself to watch him another moment. He moved with an intentional stride, a man who knew his way around animals. His actions weren't rough, just deliberate, and thoughtful, the way he'd treated her since the moment she'd opened her father's shanty door to find Two Stones on the other side.

He'd proven himself dependable. A man of his word,

there when she needed him every time. And that alone made her heart melt a little as she watched him disappear with the string of horses around the bend in the trail.

CHAPTER 6

*H*eidi was warming her hands in front of the small blaze she'd built by the time Two Stones returned with the supplies they would need that night.

He dropped his load against the rock wall. "I'll gather more wood now." He turned and strode back into the swirling snow.

Now that she had their supplies, she could ready a meal and warm drink for his return.

A quarter hour later when she handed him the cup of hot water, the smile he flashed as he dipped his face into the steam was enough to warm her insides.

"Thank you." He took a long draught, holding the cup with both hands to absorb the heat. "The warmth is good."

She turned to finish loading their plates. "Sit by the fire and warm yourself."

He obeyed, and when she handed him the plate, he patted the fur beside him. "Sit and warm yourself."

Those were nearly her own words. She glanced at the spot—far closer to him than she would have chosen. But this overhang would be tight. And she would have to sit close to stay on the fur. She didn't relish the idea of sitting on icy stone.

So she eased down beside him with her plate, keeping the soft fur he'd given her earlier tight around her like a cloak. As she ate, shivers coursed through her, and she leaned toward the fire. The icy wind still found its way under the rocky overhang, chilling her to the bone.

She glanced at Two Stones from the corner of her eye. His frame blocked some of the wind. If she scooted closer, he could protect that full side and she could glean some of his warmth. She shouldn't be so forward, though.

Yet when another gust swept through their makeshift shelter, she pushed aside her qualms. She might freeze to death before this night was over if she allowed her pride and propriety to choose.

As she leaned against his arm, he didn't seem surprised at all, just eased closer, shifting his shoulder so his hand rested behind her. Not wrapped around her waist as a suitor might, but propped on the ground, allowing her to shelter nearer his side.

The howl of the wind kept their silence from turning awkward. They were both still eating, too, and she took small bites to make the meal last longer.

When the food was gone, she pulled her fur tighter around her, closing off any gap at her neck as she snuggled deeper against his side. "Are the horses out in the weather?"

"I found trees near a cliff wall, so they will not feel much wind." The deep timbre of his voice rumbled near her ear. A delicious sound that made her feel protected.

She'd not felt protected in the arms of a man in so very long.

And hadn't actually been protected even then.

She'd need to remember to guard her heart. She might be married to this man in the eyes of God and in the town of Virginia City, but she would keep a wall around her emotions. She wouldn't let him hurt her—in body or spirit.

As they sat a little longer, the combination of his nearness, the fire crackling, the falling snow...they tightened her nerves until she could barely sit still.

Maybe talking would help.

"Tell me about your village. What was it like growing up there?"

Two Stones stared into the fire, the look in his eyes

almost tender. "It is a small town. Set near the creek between two mountains. We have lived in this place five winters, and there is still good hunting. God has blessed my people with peace and plenty."

She studied him a moment, tipping her head just enough to see him. He didn't look her way. Maybe he'd told her of his village's current location because he thought she would want to know where they were going. But that wasn't what she'd asked.

And he needed to know she wouldn't be pacified or pushed aside when she asked a question. Not anymore. "You paint a lovely picture with your words." At least, she hoped so. "But if you've lived in that valley for five years, where did you camp before that? Where did you grow up?"

He slid a look her way. It didn't seem to hold annoyance, but not humor either. He focused on the fire again. "We moved nearly every year. Always searching. Sometimes the game would leave us. Sometimes the snows would be too heavy, our people dying from the cold, even with the animal skins. The Blackfoot and Gros Ventre, they pushed us from the good camps. From the places of shelter and plenty."

He paused, as though he was back in that time, staring at a memory that darkened his mood, even years later. Would he share it? Should she prompt him? As much as she wanted to prove she was strong and capable and not willing to cower to a man, she wasn't sure she had the courage to push if he didn't offer the story on his own.

"When I was eight winters old," he said after a long pause, "I went with my cousin to gather wood around the mountain. The snow began to fall heavily, so fast that I lost my way. I could not find my cousin, no matter how I called and searched."

Heidi's chest clenched as she waited for his next words. What awful thing had happened to him at such a tender age? From the tension in his voice, it must have been bad.

"I found shelter in the cleft of the rock that night and the next. The snow stopped, and I was hungry and feared for my cousin."

"And for yourself, no doubt." She hadn't meant to speak, but the story drew her in so, the words slipped out.

The tension in his eyes eased a little as he glanced at her. "A warrior is taught not to say so. But yes, I was afraid I would not ever find my way."

His gaze moved forward again. "For two more sleeps, I wandered through the mountains. I thought I would die there." He paused, eyes clouding with the memory.

She couldn't hold in her prompting this time. "What happened?"

"I met a boy on horseback. A few winters older than me. I was so hungry, I followed him. He took me to the cabin where he lived with his mother and father and brother. Though we could not understand each other at first, they took me in and cared for me."

Two Stones's brow furrowed. "I stayed with them, learning some of their language. They gave me food and were kind."

Heidi's heart ached for the lost little boy. "You must still have been afraid and missing your family. Did you try to escape?"

Again he was silent for long enough she wasn't sure he would answer. "I knew what it was to wander lost and hungry and cold."

So he'd been too nervous to leave. "How long did you live with them?"

The knot at his throat worked, as though he was struggling to voice his answer. "After one moon passed, they thought I would always be with them. They cut my hair. Made a mattress that was my own. Two more moons passed before the snow melted in the valley."

She barely kept herself from asking if he'd tried to leave at that point. He would tell her. She had to give him time.

As though he could hear her thoughts, he spoke again. "My uncle found me when I was with the older son, hunting. He told me to come with him, and would not let me tell the boy that I was returning home."

Something in his tone wrapped a longing around her. The white family had taken him in and helped him when he'd nearly died. Taken him almost as their own, it sounded like. But how relieved he must have felt to be reunited with his own family.

Did he worry what his white friends thought of his sudden leaving, without a word of farewell or thanks? She allowed herself to turn to him fully, so he would feel her studying him. "Did you ever see them again?"

He shook his head. "My mother would not let me leave sight of our camp until we moved to a different valley. She mourned the cutting of my hair. Mourned that I had been changed to a white man."

She fought to keep from stiffening. "Because you'd spent a few months with a white family? That didn't change who you are inside."

The slight lifting at the corners of his mouth showed no sign of a true smile. And her heart ached all the more. To be torn between two worlds at such a young age...

As she looked at him now, she could see the echoes of that lost boy still in him. A glimpse into the kind yet conflicted man before her.

"Did your mother keep you away from white people after that?" She asked the question gently.

He shook his head. "There were too many, and the English I'd learned helped my people in trading. Everyone in our village called for me when they needed an interpreter."

She tipped her head. "Is that how you learned trading so well? That's what you do now, right? Find unique items for people, like specialty trading?"

A glimmer of a smile touched his eyes as he looked at her. "Something like that. I met many people when I interpreted. Most are not still here, but I do think that is where I learned to read men's intentions. To know where I could find the unusual things I am asked to search for."

He was still looking at her, but his thoughts seemed to turn inward as his mouth curved. Her gaze caught on that mouth longer than it should have. His skin was so smooth, his lips full. Not at all like Winston's thin mouth shadowed by a bushy mustache. Just one more way the two seemed as different as a Savannah summer and a Montana winter.

His voice called her back from that thought. "One of the white men I met changed me. Or rather, his God changed me." His gaze focused again, but the smile stayed at the corners of his mouth. "Dat Coulter was the first man who made me remember the English family who took me in when I was lost in the snow. He brought me to the mountain where his family was building a house."

The tenderness in his voice as he spoke brought out her own grin. "The brothers we're going to see. Those are his sons?"

He dipped his chin. "Six brothers. There was a girl, too, but she has gone from this life." Sadness touched his eyes. "Dat and Mum have left also, but they gave me much. They spoke of Creator to me, and of His sacrifice. That Jesus came to make peace between all men and Creator, making us brothers."

His expression turned earnest as he spoke of God. "I met Jesus and learned to follow His path. It is not always an easy trail—but the only place for peace. "

Heidi's throat squeezed at the intensity in his gaze. What would it be like to believe so strongly the way he did, that God cared? Was it his faith that made him so… steadfast? He possessed a kind of quiet strength. Even when she sensed his uncertainty about being Indian among white people, he still seemed rooted, his character unchanging.

It made her want to lean in and take shelter at his side. Maybe that truly would be a safe place. Her experience told her that allowing a man power over her would only bring pain.

But could Two Stones be different?

CHAPTER 7

The icy wind bit into Two Stones's cheeks as he pushed his horse through the deep snow. Beside him, Heidi huddled under the fur he'd given her, face pale and pinched from the cold. Around them, the land lay bleak, drifts piling up in the lee of rocks and ravines.

Iron-gray clouds pressed down, promising more snow to come. They'd managed two days on the trail since the last storm. This new one looked like it could delay them again. How hard could he push Heidi through the cold and wind?

She'd endured so much this past week—losing her father, nearly being attacked in Virginia City, and now day after day in this miserable cold and snow. He'd promised to protect her, to take her to a safe place. He'd not made a good start of it, that was certain. Was she losing faith in the life he'd promised she would have when they reached his people?

If they could just make it to Jericho's ranch, she would have shelter in a warm home, surrounded by good friends. Three more days. As long as the weather didn't slow them too much.

When the road leveled out near the base of the mountain they'd been descending, he nudged his horse to pick up the pace. The wind whipped around them, swirling the flakes like a thick fog, the ice crystals so cold they nearly burned.

Ahead, a dark form appeared in the distance. Two of them—men on horseback, from what he could tell through the haze. As they approached, he could make out hats the miners wore, pulled low against the blowing storm. They must be white men, coming from the main road that stretched from Virginia City to Missoula.

He and Heidi had taken a different route—one many didn't know about. More direct, and usually faster than the road these men had traveled, though the snowfall had slowed them. This was the place the two trails joined and continued on as one.

The men had spotted them, reining directly toward them.

He tensed, his hand reaching to make sure the knife

hanging at his neck was easy to reach. Then he lowered his fingers to brush the butt of his rifle in its scabbard.

He usually treated strangers as if he expected them to be friendly, but he was ready should a meeting turn dangerous. Should he do anything differently with Heidi at his side?

He glanced over at her. She was watching the strangers too, and her horse tracked close beside his own. As her gaze met his, he tried not to show any alarm.

He spoke quietly. "Stay close. I will speak."

She dipped her chin in agreement, so he turned his focus back to the men.

He'd never seen these two before, which didn't surprise him. Virginia City swarmed with new miners every time he had to travel there.

As the strangers drew near, he recognized the moment their curious expressions turned to glares. Had they just now realized he was one of the People, traveling with a white woman? Would that be enough to incite their fury? He'd seen men kill others for less. That must be it, for surely these two didn't know him individually.

One of the men reached for the rifle resting across his lap, lifting it to the crook of his arm. A position much easier to fire from quickly.

Lord, give me wisdom. The last thing he wanted was a

fight. Not only for Heidi's safety, but the stories of it would do nothing good for her reputation, being associated with him if he killed a white man.

As they all reined in, the man who'd readied his rifle spoke first. "Afternoon." His tone seemed deceptively light. His eyes flicked to Heidi, lingering there far too long.

Two Stones forced himself not to react, only to nod, acknowledging the greeting. But his body tensed, ready for anything.

The other man—the younger of the two, if the smooth skin around his eyes could be believed—looked past Two Stones to grin at Heidi, his dirty teeth flashing. "Yer that girl Tyson couldn't get hold of, ain't ya? This must be the injun that saved you." He nodded toward Two Stones, but kept his hungry gaze on Heidi.

Creator Father, put Your response in my body. Every one of his instincts wanted to spring on the two of them and slice the grimy smiles off their faces. But that wouldn't be God's leading.

He was fairly certain.

He did nudge his gelding forward a step to shield Heidi from their view. He couldn't fully block her, but at least he would make his intention plain to these snakes.

He raised his chin. "We have no business with you."

Then he started to rein his gelding away from them, motioning for Heidi to stay close.

"Maybe we got business with you." The older man's voice cut through the air before their horses managed a single step. The stranger kicked his mount hard enough, the animal leaped forward to catch them. Then the man jerked hard on his reins to stop the animal right in front of his and Heidi's horses.

Two Stones's gelding tossed its nose up in frustration, but Two Stones held his reins steady.

The fellow leveled a look on him as the younger man rode forward to position himself as back-up for his friend. "What you done to Tyson ain't right, an' I don't think we can let you leave without doin' our duty for our friend. Ain't that right, Fitz?" He tipped his chin toward his friend just enough to show those last words were aimed at him. But then his gaze slid to Heidi, and the gleam that lit his eyes made Two Stones coil to attack.

But he forced himself pause. *Should I, Lord? Is this Your way of protection?*

He sensed nothing in his spirit save a hesitation to touch these men. That might be from God, so he should try again to leave peaceably.

"I did not hurt the man, certainly not as he deserved. But I would not let him take this woman against her wishes." Should he mention their marriage? That was why Callum had wanted the ceremony, after all. To protect her in the eyes of white men. "She is my wife. I will not let you harm her."

The man's face flamed red, twisting into a foul glare. "Why, you dirty heathen." He lifted his rifle to aim.

Two Stones reacted on instinct, jerking his knife free. But he restrained himself before striking, holding back his fury by a thread. If the man moved his finger to the trigger or turned the weapon toward Heidi, he would strike.

The crack of a gunshot behind him made Two Stones jerk around. Not enough to lose sight of the two vipers, but to take in the new threat also.

His mind struggled to make sense of what he saw. The dusky haze of powder surrounded a pistol in Heidi's hand. He could just barely see her wide eyes that conflicted with the firm set of her jaw.

One of the men shifted, and Two Stones honed his focus on their threat again as he raised his knife to fling it. The men would surely retaliate against Heidi's shot.

The rifle dropped from the older man's grip, his eyes widening as his hands rose to his chest, just below his throat. His mouth dropped open, maybe from pain *and* shock, for he seemed to be struggling to believe he'd been shot.

"Walker?" His friend's voice pitched high as he

nudged his horse closer. "What's wrong? Are you hit? Is it bad?"

Both these men had lost their wits by half. If they didn't move quickly, Walker would bleed out in seconds. Maybe there was nothing they could do to save him, but there might be.

Two Stones slipped from his horse and moved to the injured man's side.

"Don't touch him!" Fitz's tone came out wild as he raised his own rifle.

Two Stones paused, letting the younger man see his hands were empty. "I'm not going to hurt him. We have to lay him down and stop the bleeding. He will not live long if we don't help."

"You've done enough. Get out of here, both of you. I'll tend him." At least his voice had lowered to a reasonable pitch now, though his eyes still looked wild.

Two Stones glanced at the injured man, who was leaning forward now, curling around his belly. He still clutched his chest, and his breathing had taken on a wheezing sound. If his airway had been hit, there was nothing they could do to help him.

He sent a quick glance toward Heidi to see how she was reacting. She'd shot a man, who would likely die from the wound. Her quick action might have saved them both from something worse, but he knew well how killing a man impacted a person.

She sat motionless in the saddle, her face stoic. At least she hadn't collapsed into tears like some women would.

He turned to the younger man again, keeping his hands out, away from his sides. "He needs help. We will leave if you wish. Or we will stay and do what we can for him."

Fitz's expression twisted into a snarl. "I told ya to git, didn't I? Get outta here before I kill ya both."

Two Stones moved back to his horse, keeping his eyes on the daft stranger. Once he'd swung into his saddle, he glanced at Heidi to make sure she was ready to ride.

She met his look with a hard set to her jaw, but he could just make out a tremble in her shoulders. She was holding together well, but she would need to release as soon as he could get her away.

He sent one more look at both men. Neither had changed position, but the injured one's shoulders rose heavily with each loud, wheezing breath. *Lord, draw him to You before his end comes.*

He motioned for Heidi to move her horse forward as he nudged his own. "Ride in front of me." He spoke just loudly enough for her to hear.

She did as he asked, and he edged his horse to keep himself between her and the men. The first time he glanced back, the younger man was pulling the other from his horse.

Two Stones eased out a breath. At least he was helping his friend. And it didn't appear he was planning to shoot them in the back.

It took far too long for them to reach the place where the path curved around a mountain, but as soon as they were completely out of sight, he moved his gelding up next to Heidi's. "There is a cabin not far from here. We can rest."

She nodded, her jaw still locked hard.

He pushed his horse into a lope, the pack horse trailing behind. The snow had been broken in this stretch by other riders, so the animals could move easier. They would get to rest soon too.

He'd wanted to cover so much more ground this day, but his wife needed to free all the struggle that churned inside her. A dry place to warm herself would help, too, especially with the coming snowfall.

He had to watch carefully for the turn-off to the old shack. The building couldn't be seen from the main road, tucked behind a cliff so it would be hidden even in the winter when the tree arms were bare. Once when he'd ridden through here after a snowfall, he'd spotted horse tracks leading off the road. He'd been curious and looking for a place to take shelter, so he'd followed the prints to the abandoned cabin.

He should lead Heidi through the trees this time, so

their tracks would not be easy to follow if the younger man came after them. For that matter, he didn't want another stranger to see their trail veering off the road and follow the prints, as he'd first done.

After they wound through a stretch of trees then rounded the edge of the cliff, the little structure stood before them, tucked against the mountainside for protection from wind and weather.

Heidi's face showed no change in her expression. She must be working to hole away her reactions to the shooting. He didn't want her to grow hard and bitter, though. Her spirit already held an edge that showed too much pain in her past. The last thing he wanted was to bring her more.

They reined in before the cabin door, and he slipped to the ground so he could help her.

She moved slowly, almost as if she was in pain. From the cold? Or the hardening inside her?

He stayed at her side as they moved toward the door. He wanted to touch her, maybe take her hand or press a palm to her back. To somehow let her know she wasn't alone. He would walk this hard path with her.

When he opened the door, it swung easier than the last time he'd been here. Someone had replaced the leather hinges, something he'd intended to do when he had the right supplies.

The air inside smelled stale. But at least it didn't

stink of animals that might have taken refuge here. He led Heidi to the place where he would build the fire. Since the cabin sat so close to the cliff, the floor was stone that extended from the base of the mountain. Someone had crafted a rock area in the corner where a fire could be built, including an opening for the smoke to escape outside.

He pulled off his coat and placed it on the cold floor. "Sit here. I'll bring in wood to make a fire."

She looked at him with a cloudy gaze. "We're stopping for the night?"

He nodded. "This is a good shelter for us. More snow is coming, and we can stay dry here."

She didn't question him further, just sat as he'd said to.

He went back out to the horses to unload their supplies, and he took the chance to lift his concerns to Creator Father. *Keep her heart soft. Do not let her close herself away from the pain. Nor push me away. You know I want to help her. I want to be the husband You would have me be to her.*

He knew nothing of how to do that. He'd spent little time with his parents for many winters now. Even in his childhood, though, he'd rarely seen his father and mother speaking as friends. Not like Dat and Mum Coulter did. Those two had spoken often, not caring who around heard them. Dat would ask her thoughts and follow her wishes in a way that brought honor to her. When Mum worried over something, he would ask her to speak of her concerns. The way they trusted each other had drawn Two Stones, even as a young man who craved a life of excitement and adventure.

He'd promised Heidi he wouldn't touch her as a husband, but he could honor her as Dat Coulter had done with Mum. *Lord, give me the right words.*

CHAPTER 8

*W*hen Two Stones finished bringing in the supplies, he knelt to build a fire in the hearth beside Heidi. She was shivering hard now but still hadn't made a sound. Hadn't really moved since she first sat. The cold likely had something to do with her trembling, but her fright even more.

As soon as he'd coaxed a flame to life, he filled the kettle with snow and nestled it among the logs to heat. He needed to see to the horses, too, and then warm food for Heidi. But maybe he could get her talking first.

He turned to face her, his knees nearly touching hers. She didn't meet his gaze, only stared past him, her body still shivering. She looked like a woman trying to be brave and fierce, but her trembling gave away the truth of her tender parts. His own chest ached to pull her close, to take on her fear and regret so she could be untainted. But she wouldn't allow that, he had no doubt. He would have to use words.

He honed his focus on her face. "You did the right thing." That wasn't quite what he'd intended to say, but it slipped out. Maybe this was Creator Father's message to her.

Her gaze flicked to his, then bounced away, her jaw setting even harder.

He pressed on, keeping his voice low and gentle. "I know shooting a man is not easy, but you saved our lives. I am grateful to you."

She turned to him then, her eyes shining and red-rimmed but still fierce. "Did you know I was married?"

He drew back a little. That was the very last thing he'd expected her to say. And why bring it up in this moment? He chose his answer carefully. "I did not. Callum spoke little about where you lived before, only how happy he was for you to come to him."

Her eyes flashed. And her chin lifted. "When my mother died, my father abandoned me at a girl's school. At least, that was what it felt like—abandonment. He took me there, then sold our house and came to this territory." She trembled so much, even her voice quivered.

But she kept going, her story twisting in his belly. "For five years I lived there. Then I caught the eye of a man from one of the best families. I thought I'd done well, forming a connection with so much advantage. He said all the right things, and my father wasn't there to tell me differently. I married him, and he turned out to be a snake. A man who took pleasure in controlling other people...me...and the men he did business with. He was only happy when we were at his beck and call." She paused for a heartbeat, her mouth pressing closed as though she were deciding what to say next.

So much he wanted to know. What had this man *done* to her to control her? Heidi seemed like such a strong, free spirit. How could anything hold her down, short of binding her with ropes? Everything in him wanted to find the viper and revenge her honor. Make him pay for every time he hurt her.

But he held his tongue so she could continue.

"He died in May." Her voice trembled again. "I'm finally free, and I *will not* be under any man's thumb again." With every word, her tone grew stronger, ringing with determination. Her eyes flared, nearly sparking now, though still rimmed red.

His anger dulled as realization spread through him. She was supposed to be safe with him, and yet she'd been afraid those two snakes were going to force her to...who knew what she thought they'd do. Take her back to the brothel owner in Virginia City maybe.

Two Stones wouldn't have let that happen, no

matter what. But his delay in acting had made her think he wouldn't stand up for her.

He leaned in so he had her full attention. He waited to speak until her eyes focused on him. "I'm sorry I made you think you had to defend yourself. That I would not protect you from those white weasels on the trail." He tapped his fingers on her arm. "You are a woman who can do anything she sets her will to. But I promised to keep you safe, and to provide all you need."

He pressed a fist against his chest. "I want with all that is in me to do these things for you." He started to rein in the emotion that surged with his words. But maybe she needed to see the fierceness. To understand how fully he intended to carry out his promise.

So he let his eyes flash. "I hate what that other man did to you. If he were not dead, I would hunt him. I would bring his actions down on his own head. Make him suffer for every day you did not feel safe and happy." He lowered his voice, but kept it hard with his anger. "I promise you this. I will be a good warrior, a good husband. I will guard you with my life. As long as I have breath, you will live in peace and plenty. Even after I am gone, I will leave you with all I can."

He waited, barely breathing as he watched her face. She gave no sign of her thoughts, but she was certainly scrutinizing him.

At last, she spoke. "And what will you require in return?"

He had to work to keep in a snort. What had her other husband required? He shook his head. "Nothing. I want only your happiness. I hope you will find it in the village of my people, but if you wish to leave, you are free to. I will keep my promise, protecting and providing for you." He might not be as free to travel for his trading if he needed to protect her in Missoula or one of the other mining towns. But he would do what he had to for her.

Not just because Callum had asked him. Not even as a matter of honor, since he'd taken her as his wife before God. But because Heidi needed him. She deserved to be safe and happy. He wanted her to be so. He *desperately* wanted it.

Maybe more than he should allow himself if he planned to guard his heart. He would have to ponder that later though. Now, Heidi needed his full support.

The sharpness of her gaze softened. She no longer seemed to be searching for the lie in his words, but maybe hoping they were true.

He let her search, not turning away as he waited.

At last, her mouth parted and quiet words slipped out. "Thank you."

Relief swept through him, nearly pulling the strength from his limbs.

She'd begun to shiver again though. Was there something he could say to ease her fears more? Maybe she simply hadn't gotten warm yet.

He reached out to touch the back of her hand. "Are you still cold?"

She nodded, a heavy tremble quivering her shoulders. "Will you...sit close? Like you did the other night?"

A layer of warmth eased through his chest. She was asking for help. Asking for him.

He moved next to her, settling close. Closer than they'd been the other night. That night, only her arm had touched his side. Now, he shifted so the length of their bodies touched. Maybe that was as far as he should go, but he wrapped his arm around her back, resting his fingers at her waist.

She didn't object, but she sat stiffly. At first. Little by little, as the crackling of the fire rose to warm the quiet around them, she eased her defenses, leaning into him.

He released a breath, letting himself enjoy the pleasure of her touch. Of her company. Of her trust.

The only problem now was remembering he'd promised to be a friend only, not a husband.

⁓

*H*eidi could still feel the memory of Two Stones's arm wrapped around her, though it had been two nights ago now. In the strength of his hold, she'd not had to face the fear of surviving in this world of men who took pleasure in hurting others. In overpowering people weaker than themselves. As she laid her head on his shoulder, she'd been free of the memory of watching the man jerk when her bullet slammed into him, the shock in his eyes turning to horror. Then pain.

Out here in the saddle, she had to squeeze her eyes shut to make the image fade. If only she could be tucked beside Two Stones again, wrapped in his comfort. But he was riding ahead of her as their horses tromped in a narrow creek. Tree-covered slopes rose up on both sides, and with the thick layer of snow concealing rocks on both sides of the water, the safest place for the horses to walk was in the creek bed.

The screech of a bird overhead drew her gaze up to where a black speck circled. After a glance at the sky, Two Stones turned back to her, his grin flashing. "We are nearly there."

He reined his gelding to the side and motioned for her to ride up next him. When she did so, he pointed to the bird. "That is Crowley, the raven my brothers keep. He sounds the presence of all who come to the ranch."

She squinted at the creature, though it was too far away to see much in the late afternoon sky. "They have a pet raven? I've heard of such, but I've never seen one."

"It's how we know when scoundrels like Two Stones are coming."

The strange voice made her jerk, and she spun to find its source in the line of trees. From the shadows stepped a man, maybe about her age. He wore a fur coat like Two Stones and a cap to match. Only his grin showed through as he came toward them.

Though he looked friendly and was probably one of the Coulter brothers, her body tensed and her hand moved to the handgun tucked at her waist. She wouldn't need it around this man. Hopefully.

Two Stones motioned for them to ride toward the newcomer, and she did so, letting her horse fall back a little as he led.

When they reached the grinning man, Two Stones reined in and slid to the ground, then stepped forward to clasp his hand. "It is good to see you, little brother."

The man pumped Two Stones's arm. "It's about time you showed up. Wait till you see what the women have planned for Christmas dinner."

His gaze moved past Two Stones. "I see you brought us a visitor."

Her mouth went dry, and her belly swooped. How would Two Stones introduce her? As his wife? Or would he simply give her name?

He stepped back, turning to include Heidi. "This is Heidi." His voice shifted both deeper and softer. "My wife." His gaze caught hers, its warmth drawing her so much that it took a moment to gather the strength to look away.

Two Stones managed it first, but the corners of his mouth tugged as he motioned to the other man. "This is Gil, one of the Coulters."

She managed to nod at Gil. "It's nice to meet you." From what Two Stones had said, Gilead was the fourth brother in line.

Gil's eyes widened, but to his credit, his shock quickly changed to pleasure. He strode forward and reached up for her hand. "By jingo, I'm pleased to shake the hand of the woman who finally won Two Stones over."

He gripped her palm firmly, like he was welcoming an old friend. She couldn't help but grin back at his exuberance, but she slid a quick glance at Two Stones to check his reaction. His brows had gathered, though he looked half-amused. And half...perturbed?

Gil stepped back to take them both in. "Come up to the house then. Everyone will want to see you both."

After Two Stones remounted, they turned up the slope, riding through the trees. Gil disappeared for a minute, then rejoined them on horseback, leading the way.

At last, they reached a clearing where the ground mostly leveled out. A cabin sat near the upper edge, with a barn downhill from it. Fresh wood covered one half of the building, clearly a very recent addition.

Through the open barn door, a man stepped out, then a boy behind him. The lad called out, "Two Stones!" and trotted toward them. "Who'd you bring with you?"

Her husband dismounted again and paused to ruffle the boy's hair before turning to Heidi, holding her horse. He must mean for her to dismount here, so she leaned forward and slid to the ground.

"Sean." Two Stones glanced from the lad to her. "This is Heidi." He didn't give their relation this time, but maybe because it wouldn't matter as much to the lad.

She smiled at Sean, ignoring the others flooding from the cabin toward them. "It's nice to meet you." This must be the nephew. And the blond girl approaching with the woman must be his sister, Lillian.

She stood back a little as two more men greeted Two Stones with hearty handshakes and claps on his shoulders. Two Stones called one of them Jericho, so the pretty blonde woman beside him who held a baby must be Dinah, the doctor who'd married Jericho. She must not be the babe's mother, for he'd said the babe belonged to Naomi, Dinah's sister.

Once they'd all greeted Two Stones, their voices quieted as their focus turned to her.

Heat crept up her face, but when Two Stones moved to her side, she managed to square her shoulders and offer a pleasant smile.

"This is Heidi." Again, his voice took on that deep, almost tender tone. "She is my wife."

CHAPTER 9

*H*eidi held her breath in the wake of Two Stones's introduction.

A few murmurs immediately sounded from those surrounding them, but she couldn't bring herself to meet any gazes. These people were almost like family to him. Did they think her unsuitable?

The woman named Dinah thrust the baby into the arms of the large man beside her. Shock struck his expression for a moment before he caught himself and adjusted the infant in his arms. A little awkward, but not as much as most men would be.

Dinah pressed through Sean and Gil, then nearly sprang on Heidi as she wrapped her arms around her. "Oh, it's so wonderful to meet you."

Heidi managed to raise her hands to return the

embrace, though it felt like she was experiencing the scene in a dream. When Dinah pulled back, she gripped Heidi's upper arms, her smile as warm as if they'd always been friends. "You must be tired. Did you come from the Salish village? Or have you been traveling much longer?"

She willed her mouth to speak and managed to say, "Virginia City."

Dinah's eyes flared wide. "Oh, you poor dear." She turned and tugged Heidi forward, keeping hold of one arm. "You must be exhausted and cold." Over her shoulder, she spoke to the others. "You boys bring in her things. Lilly, bring the baby inside. Let's help Heidi get settled."

Heidi had no choice but to follow. Honestly, the immediate acceptance eased a load from her shoulders. She sent a quick glance over her shoulder to see Two Stones's reaction to her leaving him.

He was watching her, his expression too hard to read. Not anger. Not pleasure either. It almost looked like…longing? Certainly not for her. But for what?

Dinah stopped them and looked back too. "Two Stones, come in as soon as you can. We'll help your wife settle in, but she'll want you, too, of course."

He dipped his chin, but Dinah tugged Heidi forward before she could send him any kind of message with her gaze.

The truth was, she *did* want him with her. Though she should be more than capable of managing by herself among these friendly people, his presence gave her courage. She wasn't weak. Nor fearful. If a little of those emotions churned inside her, she wouldn't let them hold her back.

But Two Stones felt like a partner. They'd endured so much together this past week. Long days in the saddle, fighting the wind and cold, and even the snow. Meeting those two men from Virginia City, then the aftermath, when he'd been her strength, there in the abandoned cabin.

He'd done so much for her. She'd tried to carry her part of the load, cooking and helping as she could. Did he regret tying himself to her yet? Probably he did, but he was too honorable to ever let her know it.

She heaved out a sigh as Dinah led her into the warm cabin. She couldn't let herself linger on thoughts like that. She had to stay focused on what lay ahead. On building the life she wanted for herself.

Surely becoming friends and allies with these women would help toward that end. Yet as she turned to answer Lillian's exuberant question about the length of their journey and what adventures they'd met, her gaze caught on the sleeping face of the precious babe nestled against the girl's shoulder.

How could she think so selfishly with such innocence before her?

Then another sensation slipped in, one that tightened her chest as her feet moved toward the babe of their own accord.

If she held to the arrangement she'd made with Two Stones, would she ever have a child of her own?

~

*A*s Two Stones stepped into the cabin and paused to let his eyes adjust to the dim interior, his gaze caught on a sight that made his heart beat faster.

Heidi.

She stood with Dinah on one side and Lillian on the other, staring up at the loft where Dinah pointed as she spoke. Did she intend for him and Heidi to sleep up there? Maybe. That was just what he'd come inside to talk over —sleeping arrangements. He needed to know how much of their agreement Heidi wanted him to tell Jericho.

But seeing her there with the little bundle of babe resting on her shoulder stole every clear thought from his mind. She looked radiant. Happy. Such a sweet smile lighting her face. Her chin rested on little Mary Ellen's head as she spoke with Dinah.

She would be such a good mother. He'd thought of that once or twice as she prepared food or anticipated a need on the trail before he asked. She was thoughtful, and as she'd finally started to trust him these last few days, her kindness had caught him unexpectedly over and over.

But holding the babe... A longing pressed in his chest, something he'd not allowed himself to even think about since Yellow Mouse refused him. He would have loved to have his own son or daughter—or both. Children he could teach and encourage.

He wouldn't have that, and he could be content with his lot. But Heidi... Was he robbing her of that dream by keeping himself from her? Maybe he should give her the choice again.

Later. When she was settled in the village with his parents and they knew each other better.

He inhaled a deep breath and eased it out as he stepped forward.

Dinah was the first to notice his presence, and she turned with a smile. "Two Stones. I was just asking Heidi if she thought the two of you could be comfortable in the loft. If not, Jericho and I can stay there while you have our room."

Heidi turned to him with wide eyes, shaking her head in an unspoken message of concern. "No. I'm sure the loft will be fine." Even as her eyes questioned him, her words were for Dinah.

He gave her an easy smile. "Yes. The loft will be fine." If Heidi wanted a room alone, he could sleep in the barn or the new bunkhouse with the rest of the men.

"Oh, good." Dinah turned to Lillian. "Will you bring down anything you'll need for the next few days? You can room with Naomi."

As if she'd recognized her mother's name, little Mary Ellen came to life on Heidi's chest with a cry. Panic flared in his wife's eyes as the babe squirmed in her arms. He'd seen Mary Ellen do this before. One heartbeat she slept, and the next, awoke with a fierce hunger. The babe was crying too loudly now for him to reassure his wife.

Dinah reached for her niece and took her, bouncing and speaking softly to Mary Ellen as she hurried her into the room where Naomi must be sleeping.

As the door closed behind her, quiet descended on them like a cloud. Heidi stared after the pair. "What happened? Did I hurt her?"

He stepped closer but stopped himself from pressing a hand to her back. "No. She startles awake when hungry. She does not think she will live another heartbeat without eating, I think." He tried to give a smile that would lighten her concern.

He had to use these moments alone to ask his question. He dropped his voice lower. "I have not told Jericho that we are not..." He scrambled for the best way to say it. "That we have not..."

She nodded quickly, making it clear she knew what he meant.

He breathed out and continued his question. "Do you wish me to speak of it? Or let them think all is as usual with us? I can sleep in the barn if I tell him."

Her eyes showed her indecision, and her bottom lip crept between her teeth—something he shouldn't allow himself to look at for long. His mind had tried to wander that direction far too many times, and the only way he could stop those thoughts was by picturing Callum. Her father had been so excited to see his daughter again. Then so worried about her safety.

That safety had to be foremost in Two Stones's mind also. Nothing else.

"I don't think they need to know. Do you?" Heidi sounded uncertain, like she very much wanted his opinion. "Do you wish to tell him? If it bothers you to hide the truth... I know he's a good friend."

Red had crept up to her ears and made splotches on her cheeks. Her pale coloring made her discomfort show so quickly. Part of him wanted to grin at her innocence, but the other part wanted to take away anything that bothered her, even this conversation.

He shook his head. "If you do not mind me sleeping

there too"—he glanced up to the loft where rustling sounded as Lillian moved around—"I can sleep on the floor."

She nodded. But before she could speak, Lillian's skirts appeared at the top of the ladder. At the same moment, the door Dinah had disappeared through opened again, and she stepped out, without the babe this time. "She'll feel better with food in her tummy." Her expression seemed clouded though. Did something about the babe's actions concern her? Or maybe her sister, Naomi.

He didn't have time to ask, for the front door opened, and the rest of the brothers trickled in, those who had been out with the herds when he and Heidi arrived. Jude first, then Jonah, still limping but walking without even a stick for support.

As the men greeted him and met Heidi, the cabin came alive with voices and laughter.

Lillian and Dinah carried plates of food to the table, and Heidi moved to help them.

The talk quickly turned to preparations for Christmas, and Sean jumped in on the topic. "We're going out to cut a tree first thing in the morning. Uncle Jericho said I can pick it out."

"Me too." Lillian sent her brother a glare.

"You can help, but I've already found the perfect one."

Miles nudged his nephew. "Actually, I've already found the perfect tree." His grin showed he was teasing the boy, and Sean responded with a pretend fist to his uncle's gut.

Miles was only five winters older than the lad, so they often scuffled in play.

Dinah stopped the commotion by calling all to the table, pointing Heidi to the seat beside Two Stones's usual chair. Though the table was large, with so many people packed around it, his knees pressed against Heidi's.

Perhaps she would have had more room if he attempted to stay on his side, but it felt good to touch her again, even in this small way. Since that night in the abandoned cabin when she fell asleep leaning against his side, her head on his shoulder, he'd craved the feeling again. Their hands occasionally brushed as she handed him her reins or a plate of food, but not the steady firm contact of her leg against his.

When Jericho bowed his head and everyone at the table joined hands, Heidi fit her palm in his as though they'd done this for years. He wrapped his fingers around hers, closing her hand in his and relishing the warmth of her.

He tried to hear Jericho's prayer, but all he could manage was his own, *Thank You, Lord, for this woman.* He shouldn't let himself be so affected by her, but how could he not when she was so near all the time? What man could resist a woman as beautiful as his wife, both inside and out?

When Jericho spoke the *amen* and Sean released his hand on one side, Two Stones had to force his fingers to unwind from Heidi's hand. She sent him a shy smile before reaching to accept a dish of potatoes from Dinah.

Could it be possible that she craved his touch as much as he did hers? Surely not. But...was there a way he could find out for certain?

CHAPTER 10

*H*eidi snuggled little Mary Ellen closer the next morning as she gently rocked in the chair by the fire. The babe was so sweet. Heidi had volunteered to hold her any time the opportunity presented.

"I think they're coming with the tree." Dinah turned from the cookstove and sent Heidi a smile.

Dinah's sister, Naomi, moved to the door. "I'll let them in." She was such a quiet woman, it'd been hard to get to know her. Maybe because Naomi had stayed in her room much of last evening and this morning.

Dinah said her sister was still recovering from the birth. But Mary Ellen was more than two months old. Shouldn't Naomi be able to participate more with the family by now? Who was Heidi to judge, though? She'd never given birth. And before meeting little Mary Ellen, she'd not realized the wonderful gift she was missing.

Part of her was thankful not to have a child from Winston.

Two Stones though... He would be such a good father. The thought of what that would require made her middle flip and her chest tighten. She couldn't do it. Not after the way it had been with Winston.

Her eyes burned even as the sound of laughter and happy voices drifted through the open door. She pressed her face into Mary Ellen's hair while she worked to pull herself back together.

"It's beautiful." Dinah spoke to the group from the doorway as Jericho appeared on the stoop, holding one side of a large evergreen. "I'm not sure how you think we'll get it inside the cabin though."

Heidi stood and moved toward them so she could better see the tree. Two Stones held the other side of the wide base, grinning when he saw her.

Something in her belly flipped at that handsome smile. This man could turn heads anywhere he went, even in a Savannah ballroom. She nearly chuckled at that notion. The older matrons would pretend to be scandalized at a black-haired native in their high-brow society. But she knew many a young woman—married or not—who would sigh and swoon every time Two Stones flashed a grin.

How in the world had she landed with such a man? In truth, it was his strength of character that appealed to her even more than his looks, considerable as they were.

His grin deepened as though he could hear her thoughts, but then he was distracted by something Jericho said.

She stepped back with the baby while they sorted how to bring in the tree and where to place it. She could join in the merrymaking by stringing popcorn or placing extra pine boughs and ribbons around the cabin for a festive touch, but having Mary Ellen in her arms gave her an excuse to simply watch. To take in the sweet innocence of it all.

This was nothing like instructing the servants where to place decorations as she'd done her first Christmas with Winston. When he came home that evening and frowned at it all, she'd escaped to her room to avoid his displeasure. By keeping to her chamber, she also managed to be absent when his mother came to rearrange everything the way a *proper* home should be decorated.

For the two Christmases after that, Winston's mother had come to oversee placement of the tree and trimmings before Heidi even began thinking about the holiday. In truth, it had been a relief to hand over the responsibility to someone Winston approved of. Mostly.

Now, she wasn't being censured for her lack of social discernment, so she could join in the decorating if she chose. But the way this family seemed to enjoy being with each other... She could watch this for days.

Sure, the brothers teased each other and sometimes ended up in a play brawl that should concern her. Yet the affection between them all was thick enough to ease any worry.

Two Stones added to banter at times, often being drawn in by one of the brothers or even Dinah. And sometimes he initiated a bit of teasing himself. Watching him made her want to join in, but she didn't dare.

After the tree was secured, he came to settle on the ladder-back chair beside her rocker, his gaze softening as he took in her and Mary Ellen. She wanted to tell him he didn't have to sit just because she was, but the warmth in his eyes and the curve of his mouth kept her from sending him away. In truth, she'd rather shoo everyone else from the room so the two of them could be alone, as they had been this last week.

Too soon though, Mary Ellen squirmed in her arms. At her first hungry cry, Naomi turned with a weary expression. Mary Ellen had already begun wailing by the time her mother took her.

"I suppose that's my cue to start on Christmas dinner." Dinah moved away from the tree. "If I know you men, you'll be hungry long before dark."

Heidi rose from the rocking chair. "I'll help you."

Time with Two Stones would have to wait. There was much to be done to prepare for Christmas.

～

*H*eidi stood at the edge of the massive wooden table, her hands covered in cookie dough as she laid out stars she'd cut from the flattened batter. The delicious aromas of cinnamon and nutmeg wafted through the air, mingling with the mouthwatering scent of roasting meat and cloves. She and Dinah had been at work for hours, with occasional help from Lillian and Naomi, and the feast was nearly ready.

A fire crackled in the hearth, casting its warm glow on the rest of the room. Everywhere she looked, the spirit of the season seemed to have taken hold—from the sprigs of holly adorning each wall peg and door frame to the massive tree that stretched the length of the wall beside the outer door.

With all the batter cut, she carried the tray of cookies to the cookstove, where Dinah stirred the apple cinnamon drink she was making.

"Those are perfect, Heidi. You have a real talent for them."

She smiled her thanks, the words feeling far better than she cared to admit. A talent for cutting star shapes from cookie dough was hardly a lifesaving ability, but the praise seemed so genuine. Perhaps she was too easily affected.

Dinah shifted to the side so Heidi could place the pan in the oven.

"Doesn't it all smell divine?" Dinah paused her stirring to inhale deeply. "There's something so magical about this time of year."

"Indeed." Heidi's chest tightened. How had she been so lucky as to find herself here, on this day, in time to experience a simple mountain Christmas so full of joy?

As though Heidi had spoken the question aloud, Dinah sighed. "The Lord certainly blessed us all by bringing you and Two Stones in time for today."

"I guess so." Even as she murmured agreement, her mind sorted through the idea. Could God have possibly orchestrated bringing her to the Montana Territory, then meeting and marrying Two Stones? Did that mean He'd intended for her father to die also?

That last thought seemed more in line with the unrelenting rod of the stern God she'd experienced in Savannah, but not the one Dinah spoke of.

Who was right? Was there a way to blend the two into a Deity who made sense? Or perhaps He was a fickle God, commanding events according to his whim and pleasure.

Her middle tightened. If that were the case, it seemed she'd somehow managed to move into His good graces in marrying Two Stones. Maybe, for the first time in her life, she could finally settle into a happy existence.

Dinah paused in the midst of her stirring, studying Heidi with a scrutinizing gaze.

Sweat prickled at her neck. What had she done wrong? Did her thoughts show?

But Dinah nodded toward the door. "Why don't you go outside and cool off? I'll watch the cookies and take them out when they're finished. You've been working all morning and you look overheated."

Heidi shook her head. "I'll stay and stir that while you go outside." She reached for the spoon in Dinah's hand.

But Dinah edged her out of the way. "I'll come out as soon as this is done. You go now." A slight frown gathered at her brow. "You're flushed. The cold air will feel good."

She *was* hot, especially standing by the stove, so she washed her hands in the basin, then headed for the door. "I'll see if anyone needs help out there." She was too warm to wear the fur cape Two Stones had given her, but she reached for the wool coat.

She stepped out into the crisp winter breeze. Relief flowed through her as the cold nipped her cheeks. She drew a deep breath, relishing the sharp clarity of the air as it filled her lungs.

She paused to take in her bearings, her gaze lifting to the distant mountains that rose through a gap in the tree line. There was a majestic beauty in those peaks that crept inside her, weaving its way to her very core. In this place she could be free. No matter the challenges of survival, at least she had the same chance as the next person.

She brought her focus to the clearing around her. The barn seemed quiet now, though there had been plenty of activity around it each time she'd stepped outside for water.

She slipped on her coat and started toward the structure, the snow crunching under her boots. The older section of barn stood weathered and rusty, a testament to the years it had endured and the many, many snowfalls. The new construction had its own walk-thru door. That must be the bunkhouse Dinah had mentioned, where the younger brothers and Sean slept.

When she reached the open barn door, she peered inside, hesitating for a moment as her eyes adjusted to the darkness within.

"Hello?" No voices answered, only the rustle of animals in the stalls. Where had everyone gone? No one had said they were going to check on the herds. Might they have ridden down to the creek for something?

As she walked into the shadowy interior, her footsteps echoed around her, amplifying the quiet. A cow offered a quiet moo as she passed one of the enclosures, and she nearly jumped at the sound. She moved toward the animal. "Hello there."

The cow munched hay and eyed her.

The hairs on the back of Heidi's neck stood on end, and she couldn't help but glance over her shoulder, half-expecting to see someone—or something—coming in from the daylight outside.

But there was nothing, only the light streaming through the open door.

She turned and started back that way. Her gelding and Two Stones's horses had been penned in the corral outside. They would welcome attention, no doubt.

She left the barn and approached the corral, where the three horses grazed on hay. Two Stones's riding horse flicked its short tail slowly, the natural movement easing some of the tension in her chest.

Her own gelding gave a soft snort and wandered toward her. She met him at the fence, reaching through to rub the flat part of his forehead, then his favorite spot on his jaw. "You're such a good boy."

The horse nuzzled her arm affectionately, and she moved to rub his neck.

The crunch of boots on snow sounded behind her, and she turned to see which of the Coulters approached.

Her breath caught at the figure emerging from the shadows of the nearby trees.

The companion of the man she'd shot. Her mind scrambled for his name. Fitz? Walker was the older man, the one she'd killed. Her throat burned as it always did with that though.

"Remember me?" His growl dripped with anger.

Heidi's heart pounded loud in her ears. "Why are you here?" And why hadn't she tucked her pistol in her waistband before leaving the cabin? She'd felt so safe surrounded by the Coulters, but this proved that danger truly lurked everywhere.

He took another menacing step toward her. "You're going to pay for what you did."

Her instincts screamed at her to flee. Could she make a run for it?

No. He would shoot her well before she reached the barn.

So she held her ground. Panic threatened to engulf

her, but she fought hard to keep it at bay. Her survival depended on her ability to think clearly.

He halted two strides away from her, close enough that the rifle would kill no matter which part of her his bullet struck.

"What do you want?" Her voice trembled, no matter how much strength she tried to force into it.

His smirk returned. "Justice. For Walker. And probably a nice little reward for taking you back to Virginia City."

Her heart thundered so hard she couldn't breathe. "I'm not going with you. No matter what you do." She would rather die than end up in a brothel.

But maybe…she managed a tiny breath. If she could delay him, perhaps Two Stones or one of the others would come back and help her.

God, if You're up there. If You care at all, help me. Please. Send Two Stones. She lifted the silent prayer even as her attacker edged forward.

"Don't think your injun is gonna save you this time neither." He glared. "He's busy with a little distraction I set up. Plenty long enough for you an' me to get far away from here."

Distraction? What did he mean?

He motioned to the snow beside her. "Git to the ground. On yer belly. Hands behind yer back."

With that rifle pointed at her, she didn't have a choice.

"If you give me even a blink o' trouble, I'll kill you as fast as you killed Walker. No question about it. I'd rather have the reward from Tyson for bringin' you back to Virginia City, but if you make it hard, I'll be done with ya here an' now." The ice in his tone said he meant every word.

She slowly dropped to her knees where he'd pointed. She just needed to buy time. The snow seeped through her skirts in seconds, and when she lay flat on the ground, her legs burned from the cold. Thankfully, her coat slowed the wetness reaching her upper body, but she would feel it soon enough.

"Arms behind you." The man's bark made her jerk.

She obeyed, and when he gripped her wrists with a rough hold, the powerless feeling that swept through her felt far too familiar. The weight of despair nearly suffocated her, bringing back every memory she'd tried to block out. Every time Winston...

She couldn't breathe. She couldn't think. *God, help me! Help me.* Her prayer was nearly smothered beneath the deafening roar of her own fear.

And as the cold darkness closed in around her, her world closed to a single thought. *Send Two Stones. Please.*

CHAPTER 11

*T*wo Stones coughed from the acrid smoke as he scooped another armful of snow and threw it on the billowing flames engulfing the shed. The fire only licked higher into the gray winter sky.

Snow still blanketed the ground all around them. The shed catching fire couldn't be an accident. Was someone trying to get to the crates of sapphires stored inside? But why would they set fire instead of simply stealing the treasure?

His blood turned to ice as realization struck. A distraction.

He spun, staring toward the house, though he couldn't see it for the trees.

The women. Heidi and Dinah and Naomi—and the baby—were alone in the cabin. Vulnerable.

"Jericho!" Two Stones turned once more to find his friend, yelling over the roar and crackle of the blaze. "I'm going to the cabin! The women."

Jericho's face showed question for half a heartbeat, then his eyes widened as the same truth sank in for him. He turned and yelled something to Jude.

Two Stones sprinted toward the house, and as he left the burning building behind, the sound of Jericho's steps pounded behind him. It usually took a quarter hour to walk the distance from the storage shed to the cabin, and they were traveling uphill this direction. He feared he didn't have fifteen minutes. He had to get to Heidi before someone hurt her.

Who would have gone through so much to distract them all? Immediately, an image of the younger man they'd met on the trail flashed through his mind. Fitz. Would he have traveled all the way out here for vengeance on his friend? He'd seemed to only want them to leave. But when he'd had a chance to think, had he changed his mind?

Could the brothel owner from Virginia City have come all this way for Heidi? He was likely desperate for beautiful young women, and she certainly fit that description. But this far?

He could have sent someone. A hired gun.

Urgency propelled his legs faster. He had to get

there before they hurt Heidi. *Creator Father, place Your hands around her to protect. Do not let them harm her.*

The clearing appeared through the branches ahead, and he could just barely make out the outline of the barn. He slowed to stop at the edge of the trees so he could see what was happening before he entered the clearing.

There was no sign of movement except from the horses in the corral. The animals stared toward the trees to his right.

His gaze caught a motion in that direction, and his breath closed off. That was Fitz, heaving something onto a horse.

A body.

Two Stones tucked farther behind the tree, waving to stop Jericho as he reached him.

He did his best to quiet both his breathing and his racing heart as he focused on the bundle Fitz was adjusting on his horse's shoulders. That was the skirt Heidi had been wearing.

Anger surged through him. Had the man killed her? He had to assume she was alive. Had to act quickly to save her.

Using the stealth his father and uncles had taught him as a child, he moved through the trees around the edge of the clearing, closing in on Heidi's attacker.

But the man must have seen him, for he swung onto

his horse behind Heidi's body and spun the animal, then dug in hard as they lurched into the woods. Just before the trees hid them, he caught sight of Heidi's legs, kicking furiously.

Relief took away a single layer of fear from his chest, but didn't cool his anger. She was alive but still very much in danger.

He took off toward the horses in the corral.

"Wait. We need rifles," Jericho yelled as he sprinted toward the house.

Yes. He could get the horses while Jericho gathered guns.

It took too long for him to grab bridles from the barn, then slip them on his and Heidi's geldings in the corral. Jericho's pinto was pastured down the hill, so he could ride Heidi's horse for now.

Two Stones leaped onto his mount bareback as Jericho arrived with the weapons.

Dinah stood in the cabin doorway, her worry clear in the outline of her shoulders. "We'll be praying."

He took the rifle and shot bag from Jericho, then plunged his heels into his horse's side. Fitz might have a head start on them, but at least the snow would help them follow his tracks at a run.

Maneuvering downhill in the snow wasn't easy—for them or the horses—but he used every one of his senses to keep his gelding on the trail at a swift canter. The bitter cold stung his face, and branches caught them several times. He ignored it all, focusing on catching up with Heidi and her attacker.

They were gaining ground, they had to be. But the slope became steeper as they followed a route so rocky, the horses kept slipping on ice.

Two Stones eyed the ravine at the bottom. If he remembered right, there was no way to cross it. The man would have to turn left or right. He would likely go right, toward the Mullan Road with access to Virginia City and all the other mining towns.

They could turn now and cut him off—if he took that route. *Lord, don't let me choose wrong.*

Two Stones glanced back at Jericho and pointed to the shortcut he was thinking of.

Jericho nodded. "Let's try it." They would need to pick their way carefully, but it was their best chance of heading off the man.

Guide our horses' steps. Let us reach her. Protect Heidi.

He kept up his prayers as he reined his horse toward the steeper section. The animal snorted as its hooves slipped on an icy stone, but Two Stones held his reins steady and leaned back to help the horse keep its balance. One misstep could mean disaster, but God had control over their horses' movements.

And the actions of Heidi's captor.

Thank You that You have already won this battle. Your power is greater than the plans of any man.

At last, they reached level ground beside the ravine. He peered down at the frozen creek far below, then turned his gaze back to the narrow path they were on now. Surely the man had gone this direction instead of turning left at the ravine, which would take him deeper onto Coulter land.

"There."

Two Stones turned to look where Jericho pointed. Fresh tracks moved along the base of the slope ahead of them.

He pushed his horse into a trot as they followed the prints. This was as fast as they could maneuver on the narrow ledge.

He had to fight urgency in his chest. God had already won the battle. They simply had to arrive when the Lord planned for them to.

As the ravine grew shallower and its sides not as steep, the tracks moved down to the creek bed. Two Stones slowed and studied the path ahead. Should they stay up on the bank or follow Fitz's trail down?

"We might be able to see him from above if we stay here." Jericho's quiet words stated exactly what Two Stones had been wondering.

He nodded. "Let's try it." They might have to move slower to watch for sign that the man had tried to ride up the far bank. But it would be worth the chance to have the advantage if he'd stayed down in the ravine.

Two Stones pushed his horse forward, ducking beneath snow-laden branches. The cold air burned his lungs, but that was nothing compared to the pain Heidi must be experiencing. *Father, protect her. She's in Your hands.*

They were getting close now—he could feel it. Every fiber of his being strained toward Heidi. If that snake had harmed one hair on her head...

A gunshot rang out, echoing through the silent forest.

Two Stones's heart seized. *No.*

He drove his heels into his horse's sides, racing along the top of the ridge. In the ravine below, a flash of movement made him slow.

A horse bucking. That was Fitz atop the animal, struggling to control it. And Heidi...

A form lay on the ground, a short distance from the flailing horse. That was her skirt.

And she wasn't moving.

He couldn't breathe, couldn't move. His mind knew he had to get to her, but his body wouldn't obey.

The bucking horse reared, then tumbled backward. Man and horse screamed together, and Two Stones's own belly lurched.

The horse landed on its back, squashing Fitz

beneath his saddle. Then the animal scrambled onto its side, pausing for a single heartbeat before heaving up to its feet.

Fitz still lay in the snow. A second motionless body.

Two Stones finally shifted into action. He jumped from his horse, keeping hold of his rifle, then scrambled down the side of the ravine. He had to help Heidi. If there was any spark of life left in her, he would coax it back to a flame.

Even as he ran, the realization flicked in his mind. He had no ability to breathe life or death. Only the Creator could do so. *Fan the spark to flame, Lord.*

Jericho reached the bottom of the slope just behind Two Stones, and he headed toward the man, leaving Two Stones to focus on Heidi. His wife.

"Heidi?" He couldn't breathe as he approached her, slowing the final step so he could drop to his knees beside her.

She lay on her side, facing away from him. And she didn't respond. No movement at all.

He laid a hand on her shoulder. "Heidi. Wake up."

Her coat was wet through, and he brushed her hair away from her neck so he could feel for the beat of life.

Yes!

The pulse was light and fast, but blood still pumped through her.

He gave her shoulder a gentle nudge. "Can you wake, Heidi? We need to get you warm."

She gave a small moan, but her eyes stayed closed.

He had to get her back to the cabin. He scanned the length of her, checking for signs of broken bones. Her hands were still tied behind her back, so he sliced the cord quickly, then took more care as he adjusted her arms. Did he dare turn her?

Warmth was what she needed more than anything.

He turned to check on Jericho, and his friend was straightening from the man on the ground. His face wore a grim expression as he shook his head. "He landed on a rock. He's bleeding from his head, but I think it might have snapped his neck. He's gone."

Two Stones's belly twisted. He should feel relief. He did, for Heidi no longer had to fear the man. But to die in such a way…there was no honor in it. And he'd lost his chance to come to Creator Father.

He needed to focus on Heidi now. "I have to get her back to the cabin. She's cold and not waking."

Jericho surveyed the scene, then started toward the side of the ravine they'd descended. "I'll bring the horses down."

While he waited for his friend to find a place where the animals could descend, Two Stones removed his fur coat and lifted Heidi enough to wrap it around her. Her own coat was soaked through, and her dress beneath too. This would have to do until he could get her back to the warm house and dry clothes.

When Jericho reached them with the horses, Two Stones mounted his gelding and Jericho lifted Heidi up to him. He tucked her close in front of him. Her body had begun to shiver now—a good sign. She was coming back to life, though she still hadn't opened her eyes.

"Ride on." Jericho stepped away. "I'll load the body on his horse if I can. If not, we'll come back for him later. Either way, I won't be far behind."

Two Stones paused long enough to meet his friend's gaze. "Be careful."

Jericho dipped a small nod. "Get your wife home."

Two Stones spun his gelding and urged him as fast as the ground would allow, the words echoing through his thoughts.

Yes. Heidi *was* his wife, and wherever she was would be home for him. From this day forward. What would it be like to have a real marriage with her?

Even as the question seeped in, reality pushed through the picture. He lived on the trail, and he couldn't force that life on her. Not only would she never feel at home, but the dangers he faced would be so much more treacherous for her—a woman in such a wild land full of even wilder men.

She would be safer with his family. Could he stay there with her? Not when he'd promised to leave her alone. His chest clenched. Was there a way to keep his word and still make a life for her?

Only if she changed her mind about their marriage, and only Creator Father could accomplish such a feat. *Lord, if it be Your will…*

CHAPTER 12

*H*eidi awoke to a throbbing ache in her feet and legs. The soft mattress cradled her weary body, so different from the frozen ground where Two Stones had found her the day before.

That awful day.

She'd bounced and fought with every step the horse took, though she was bound and gagged, laying over the mount's shoulders with all the blood pooling in her head.

Fitz had grown tired of her struggling and dumped her on the ground so he could shoot her. She'd squeezed her eyes shut and waited for the slam of the bullet in her body.

That blast of gunfire echoed through the snowy landscape and through her head.

But she'd not been shot.

Her body had already passed the point of shivering, her hands and legs nearly numb as she lay in the snow. Then strong arms had lifted her, out of the snow and onto another horse.

Two Stones. His warmth had wrapped around her, cradling her in his strength. Not even the miserable cold could steal away her relief at being in his arms.

When he'd carried her into the cabin, Dinah had insisted he bring her into the room she and Jericho shared. Two Stones had laid Heidi on this bed, and Dinah changed her to dry clothes, then piled blankets on her, tucking them around her shivering form.

Again and again, Two Stones had come with heated stones wrapped in cloth, placing them at Heidi's feet and hands. The heat seeped into her skin, burning as it melted away the chill in her bones.

Each time she'd opened her eyes, his dark gaze searched her face, relief flooding his features when she managed a weak smile. At last, he had sat on the bed, holding her close. Finally, she had stopped shivering, and blessed sleep claimed her.

Now, as daylight shone through the window, the warmth under the covers was almost too much, the tingling in her extremities bordering on pain as feeling returned.

Beyond the bedroom door, voices murmured, the

clanking of pans and the thump of boots indicating the others must be gathering for the missed Christmas meal. The scents of roasted meat and warm bread wafted in, Heidi's stomach rumbling in anticipation.

A gentle knock sounded before the door creaked open. Two Stones entered, his hair neatly braided, wearing a rich blue shirt.

"Good morning." His warm eyes studied her. "How are you feeling?"

"Much better, thanks to you." Her voice rasped, so she cleared her throat.

A smile touched his gaze. "Let's get you to the table then."

She pushed the blankets aside and started to rise. Thankfully, Dinah had changed her into a dress, not nightclothes. When her stocking feet touched the hard floor, the shooting pain made her wince.

Two Stones stepped forward and lifted her in his arms.

"I can walk." Even as she protested, she curled against his chest.

"I know." He slid her a look. "But allow me this."

She did, relaxing against him and resting her hands on his shoulders. His strength surrounded her, his heat seeping into her weary body. She felt utterly safe.

This man who had vowed to protect her, who asked for nothing in return, embodied everything she so desperately craved, even if she hadn't allowed herself to admit it. And God had brought him to save her, not just that first day, right before her father died, but yesterday too, when he'd lifted her numb body out of the snow.

She could see Almighty's hand, guiding them together. Tears pricked her eyes as she finally allowed herself to believe it—that God had worked all things for her good these past weeks.

And maybe He had before that too, if she thought back. She would have to spend time talking with Him when she was alone. For now, she offered up a silent *Thank You* that she meant from the very depths of her soul.

Two Stones settled her into her chair at the table, then lingered beside her as the Coulters bustled about, carrying heaping plates of roasted deer meat, potatoes, and warm biscuits.

"I hope you're hungry, Heidi." Dinah placed a dried apple pie in front of her. "Lilly and I have been at it again this morning, cooking even more to go with what we made yesterday."

Heidi smiled. "It smells wonderful. Thank you, truly. All of you." She glanced around the table, taking in the circle of welcoming faces. "I don't know how I'll ever repay your kindness."

"No need for that." Jericho shook his head. "We're

just thankful you're here." His unspoken *alive* lingered in her mind.

She ducked to hide the threatening tears. She had lost so much, but she'd gained something precious. Not just Two Stones, but also this family who loved him as one of their own. And they were extending the same to her.

As they began the belated Christmas feast, laughter and light filled the little cabin. The food tasted every bit as good as it smelled, and she relished every bite, though she grew full far too soon.

Even before most of them had finished eating, Sean's voice rose above the rest. "Can we open our gifts now?"

Miles nudged him. "Jericho said we have to clean out the barn first. You get started and we'll be right behind you."

Sean scrunched his nose at him. "You go first. See if I come help you."

She grinned at the pair, and her face kept the smile as the children were handed their first presents. Jericho and Dinah had given Lillian a doll with blonde hair to match her own. Its beautiful red dress also matched the coat they gave her pup, Apple. The next present Lillian opened came from Naomi—a red dress matching the clothing for her doll and pup. This one was definitely Lillian's size though, decorated with beautiful lace that would make her look like a princess.

The girl's eyes shone with pure joy as she thanked the quiet woman. "It's perfect. More than I ever dreamed."

Naomi squeezed her hand across the table. "It was my pleasure. The color will be lovely on you."

The chaos grew as the others shared gifts with each other, occasional squeals and laughter rising over the hum of excited voices.

Heidi glanced over at her husband. If only she could give him something special for Christmas, to show him what he meant to her. She had nothing. Except...

Two Stones met her eyes as he reached into his pocket and pulled out a small leather pouch. "I have something for you." A shy smile touched his lips.

She took the bag, searching his face for any sign of what it held. He revealed nothing, so she reached in with two fingers and pulled out the tiny metal piece.

It was a delicate gold ring was set with a brilliant blue stone.

She blinked back her tears and lifted the ring. It glimmered in the firelight, the blue gem deep and dazzling.

"It's sapphire. Mined from our mountains." He spoke softly. "Like your necklace."

Heidi's vision blurred, joy and gratitude swelling

within. "It's beautiful." And it added to the greatest gift he could have given her—him.

She hadn't brought herself to wear the necklace yet. She needed more time to ponder all that Papa meant with that gift. But this one...

"Here." Two Stones took her hand gently, then slid the ring onto her finger. A perfect fit.

Heidi stared at it, emotions swelling in her chest. "Thank you," she whispered.

Two Stones's thumb brushed over her knuckles, the tender touch sending a tremor through her.

He must have thought the shiver came from cold, for he pushed his chair back. "I'll take you to bed. You still need rest."

She allowed him to lift her again, and the others called "Merry Christmas" as Two Stones carried her back to the bed chamber. She would walk the next time she got up, but for now, being cradled in her husband's arms felt too good.

After he eased her down on the edge of the bed, she patted the mattress beside her. "Sit with me?"

He did so, but now she couldn't quite meet his gaze. How to say this?

She inhaled a breath for courage and began. "I can't thank you enough. For coming after me, for saving my life. You've shown me such care and kindness when I least deserved it."

Two Stones brushed a strand of hair from her cheek. "You deserve all of it and more."

Heidi bit her lip. "I know we married because my father begged it of you, but I want our marriage to be real. In every way." She flushed. "When the time is right."

She couldn't stand not seeing his reaction, so she managed a glance up at him.

Joy sparkled in his dark eyes, along with something richer. He reached for her hand and raised it to his lips, as he had at the end of their wedding ceremony.

But this time he kissed her palm, a feeling far more intimate than when he'd kissed the backs of her fingers.

"I will wait as long as needed." His gaze was so earnest. "You are a gift beyond measure."

A gift?

Her?

After all the rejection and abuse she'd endured at the hands of her previous husband, could anyone consider her that?

And yet Two Stones did. Rather than deny the truth of his words, she let herself sink into his eyes, losing herself in the love there. And when he angled toward her, she raised up to meet him partway.

His mouth caressed hers, a touch so gentle, so reverent, her heart overflowed.

God had blessed her to overflowing.

When he pulled away, he scooped her into his arms, settling her on his lap. She curled into his chest with a contented sigh. "Merry Christmas, husband."

"Merry Christmas, wife." His voice rumbled in her ear, soothing all the way through her. His strength surrounded her, his warmth seeping into her bones.

And in the circle of his arms, she'd finally found home.

I pray you loved Two Stones and Heidi's story!

Jude's book is next in the series, and I think you'll love it!

Turn the page for a sneak peek of *Protecting the Mountain Man's Treasure*, the next book in the Brothers of Sapphire Ranch series!

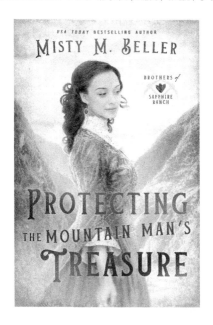

CHAPTER ONE

The sun hung low in the sky, casting a golden glow over the bustling streets of New York City as Jude Coulter stepped out of the ornate office building. The marble and opulence felt foreign compared to the rugged mountains of his family ranch in the Montana Territory he knew so well.

"Have an excellent day, Mr. Coulter." The uniformed man who'd opened the door for him gave a half bow before closing it behind him.

Jude nodded his thanks, though the fellow had already disappeared. He tightened his grip on the carpet bags in each hand and started down the cascade of steps to the street.

It now seemed foolish to carry so many gold coins with him instead of having them sent to the train station by delivery wagon—in padded unmarked crates of course, the same way he'd brought the sapphires from their ranch all the way to the city.

He'd been worried about traveling with so much money though. It seemed safer to always have it with him. Especially since it wasn't too much for him to carry himself.

Yet perhaps these two bags made him stand out from others.

The cab he'd ridden in from the train station still waited for him on the street, as he'd instructed. When he reached the rig, he climbed in. Did the driver wonder what was in the bags? Jude hadn't had them when he first hired the man back at the train station, so their presence now would surely raise a question in his mind.

"The station, sir?" The wiry man on the bench looked back at Jude, brows raised.

"Yes. Thank you." He should have thought to give the direction, not expect the fellow to read his mind. He was out of his element here, no question.

The driver called to the horse, and the cab lurched forward, weaving into the flow of traffic.

Flow might be a generous word. More like a swirl.

Hordes of people and vehicles moved in every direction, their sounds melding into a discordant chorus. Shouts. Calls from street vendors. Horses snorting and shod hooves clopping against cement and stone. Wagon wheels, the creaking of so many harnesses. Too many sounds to dissect, and the effort tightened his body until his head pounded.

He closed his eyes and brought up a memory of the creek on their ranch, the peaceful murmur as it flowed over rocks. That's where they'd first found the sapphires. Blue and pink stones lying visible among the many brown and gold-flecked pebbles.

The gold wasn't real, of course. Just pretty mica. Which is why the place wasn't overrun with miners like other parts of the Montana Territory. But Dat had realized the significance of the other colored stones.

Jude had loved working with him back then. Then when Dat and Mum passed on, he'd spent long days by himself at the creek, searching for more sapphires. Digging in the areas where they'd found the most.

Mining the gems that Dat had treasured became Jude's special role. His contribution to the family. His responsibility.

"Here we are." The driver's words sounded just as the cab jolted to a stop. The vehicle rocked as the horse found its footing.

Jude straightened and scanned the busy station. Even more people packed in here than on the street. He gripped his bags and stepped from the cart.

He had to set down one of the satchels to pull out payment for the driver. "Thank you. Will that suffice?" He'd added another dollar to the amount the man had quoted for the round trip.

The cabby's teeth flashed as he nodded. "That'll do."

Jude re-secured his grip on both bags, and turned toward the end of the station where he'd left his other piece of luggage in locked storage.

The porter who'd helped him before was speaking to a dark-haired woman, so Jude waited his turn. As the man gathered her luggage, she was asking about trains heading west, and the porter was explaining the different options available.

Though she didn't say so exactly, her words sounded like she was traveling by herself. That seemed odd, but maybe things were done differently in the city.

She was a pretty thing. Not bigger than a minute, with dark hair pulled back in a tight knot. Though she was asking questions, she seemed to know exactly what answers she needed. As though the man was simply filling in gaps of her knowledge.

"Thank you, sir. Good day." Her final words held a light accent that hadn't showed in her earlier questions. Not strong, but...different.

When she turned to walk past Jude, she offered a polite smile. Her dark eyes held just a hint of a slant, a look that made her beauty even more striking than he'd first thought.

He tipped his chin in greeting. Should he also say hello?

She passed before he could decide, so he turned to the porter.

"How can I help you, sir?" The man looked like he was forcing pleasantness he didn't feel. Dealing with strangers all day couldn't be easy.

"I have a bag in holding." Jude nodded toward his piece. "That one. Coulter is the name."

The porter nodded and pulled the carpet bag out of the fenced area. "May I see your ticket, please?"

Jude set down his load and pulled the stub from his pocket, then handed it over.

The porter nodded. "Very good." He handed over the bag, then pointed to a large number suspended from the metal rafters by the train tracks. "You'll be leaving from platform number three."

After thanking the man, Jude meandered toward the spot. A crowd had already gathered, but he worked his way around the edge until he reached a place to stand and wait on the platform.

It would be a quarter hour before the train arrived, but he'd wait here. The sooner he boarded the train, the sooner he would get to the Montana Territory.

And home.

He'd never realized how important the peace and quiet of the mountain wilderness had become to him.

Angela Larkin watched the man from a distance, doing her best to keep a bored look that showed neither the target of her gaze, nor the way her heart pounded louder than the incoming train. She would likely have a long journey, unless she could learn what she needed during one of the early legs. If she had to travel all the way to the western territories, she was prepared to do so.

She carried a significant responsibility with this assignment, and she would fulfill her part no matter what it required. She took a deep breath and smoothed the folds in her dress. She was more than capable.

Lord, guide me. This would be a delicate dance of deception and trust, and she had every intention of leading.

The arriving passengers had finished disembarking, and the porter began calling for boarding to begin. She followed the surge of people moving toward the cars. One thing she'd learned early on in this city was to go with the flow when possible. You could weave your way through as you needed to, but you'd reach your goal much faster by working with people than trying to outsmart them. That motto generally proved accurate both in traffic, and in accomplishing each mission she was assigned by the central office.

As she boarded and made her way into one of the

passenger cars, she did her best to keep the target in view. She stopped in the same car he did, and slid into a seat three rows behind him. His back was to her, but that was fine. He wouldn't see how often she watched him.

When all had been loaded, the train shuddered, then started forward with an unsteady rocking motion. An older man still standing in the aisle stumbled. Her target started to jump up to help the man, but he grunted and sank onto his bench before Coulter could act.

As the train picked up speed and the view through the windows changed from city streets to rolling countryside, the rocking of the car eased into a smoother rhythm.

She reached for the book in her bag, but she'd barely opened to her marker when a movement ahead caught her notice.

Coulter rose to his feet and stepped into the aisle. He paused for a moment, gripping his seat back as he found his balance with the movement of the train.

She kept her focus on the page before her, watching him from the edge of her gaze. Should she look up and smile? Sometimes it was better for the target to be aware of her, seeing her as just another passenger. Especially if she had a convincing backstory. More often though, she succeeded best when she could fade into the background.

So she kept her gaze down, reading the same line over and over as he moved slowly down the aisle toward her. The outside platform was through the door behind her, and he probably wanted air.

As he passed beside her, a violent jerk shook the train.

Gasps filled the air, and Jude grabbed onto her seat back to keep from tumbling. A scraping sounded above her, and she spun to see its source.

"Watch out." Jude lunged behind her, diving for a box that slid off the upper shelf. A woman screamed.

Angela lost sight of him as he pulled the box sideways, away from the elderly woman on the bench behind Angela.

A crash sounded, and she leaped from her seat to make sure Jude hadn't hurt himself.

The woman screamed again, the one he'd just saved with his quick actions.

But Jude himself lay on the floor, his head slumped against the side of the crate. Eyes closed.

"Mr. Coulter!" Angela sprang to his side, dropping to her knees.

Lord, don't let him be dead. His chest rose with a breath, so she called again, daring to touch his shoulder for a gentle shake. "Mr. Coulter."

He didn't blink. No sign of alertness.

His head was pushed forward by the box, his chin pushed into his neck. With one hand under his head, she pulled the crate out and laid him flat on the train floor.

He still didn't open his eyes.

Her mind scrambled for what to do next. She needed help. She was skilled at many things, but her medical knowledge wasn't nearly strong enough for this situation.

She looked up at the worried faces gathered around them. "Is anyone a doctor?"

No matter what, she couldn't let anything happen to Jude Coulter until he led her back to the source of the sapphires he'd just delivered.

A great deal more than her job depended on her succeeding in this mission.

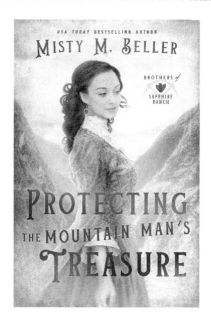

Get PROTECTING THE MOUNTAIN MAN'S TREASURE, the next book in the Brothers of Sapphire Ranch series, at your favorite retailer!

Did you enjoy Two Stones and Heidi's story? I hope so! **Would you take a quick minute to leave a review where you purchased the book?** It doesn't have to be long. Just a sentence or two telling what you liked about the story!

To receive a free book and get updates when new Misty M. Beller books release, go to https://mistymbeller. com/freebook

ABOUT THE AUTHOR

Misty M. Beller is a *USA Today* bestselling author of romantic mountain stories, set on the 1800s frontier and woven with the truth of God's love.

Raised on a farm and surrounded by family, Misty developed her love for horses, history, and adventure. These days, her husband and children provide fresh adventure every day, keeping her both grounded and crazy.

Misty's passion is to create inspiring Christian fiction infused with the grandeur of the mountains, writing historical romance that displays God's abundant love through the twists and turns in the lives of her characters.

Sharing her stories with readers is a dream come true for Misty. She writes from her country home in South Carolina and escapes to the mountains any chance she gets.

Connect with Misty at www.MistyMBeller.com